PASS IT ON!!

WINNIFRED HOLLY

To order additional copies of this book, contact:
Xlibris
844-714-8691
www.Xlibris.com
Orders@Xlibris.com

ISBN: Softcover   978-1-6641-6070-5
         EBook   978-1-6641-6069-9

Print information available on the last page

Rev. date: 02/25/2021

This book is dedicated to my Gram Charlene. She plays such a huge role in my life and encourages me to be the best I can be. I cannot thank her enough for all she's done and all the sacrifices she's made for me. Thank you to my whole family for loving and supporting me. I am sorry I couldn't write individual messages in here to each of you; if I were to do so, I'd never stop. There is an unbelievable amount of unconditional love and support radiating from all of you. I know I wasn't the typical kid, with my head in a notebook all the time. I love all of you from this world to way past the moon and all the stars.

Some teachers of mine whom I would like to send a shout-out to are Mrs. Ross, Mrs. Wilson, Mrs. Rohaley, Mrs. Conaway, Mrs. Edie, and Mrs. DeShields. They helped me so much through the formative years of my life. However, there are two teachers who helped me out the most: Mrs. Ring and Mr. Davis. Mrs. Ring helped me develop my writing, and I was in a writing club that she was in charge of. I cannot thank her enough. Mr. Davis has gone above and beyond by encouraging me to be myself all the time and to pursue what I love to do. He is my favorite teacher, and he does not get enough credit for what he does. I have never seen a teacher who is as dedicated and hardworking as he is. He is a special teacher, and I am more than grateful to know him. Thank you, all. I would not be doing this without all of your support. :)

CONTENTS

CONTENTS

As both a writer and a reader, I have always wished that authors would include more of the things that inspired them and encouraged them to write. I wished they'd tell us about the things that helped them write, such as songs they listened to while writing (or if the writer likes silence), quotes they thought about, etc. So that's what I am going to include here.

Here are some of the songs I listened to while I wrote. (Yes, I wrote them down. My writing process is very unique and special to me.) They are in no particular order.

- ★ The entirety of Melanie Martinez's music (She's my favorite musician and I would absolutely love to meet this amazing person someday.)
- ★ "Your Face is Like a Melody" – Lana Del Rey
- ★ "Thinking about You (Sometimes)" – Robert
- ★ "Mad at Disney" – Salem Ilese
- ★ "KOOL" – BENEE
- ★ "Isolate" – Sub Urban
- ★ "Animal" – Neon Trees
- ★ "My Type" – Saint Motel
- ★ "Broken" – lovelytheband
- ★ "Are You Bored Yet?" – Wallows
- ★ "Mona Lisa" – Limi
- ★ "Walk But in a Garden" – LLusion ft. Mxmtoon
- ★ "Make Me Cry" – Noah Cyrus ft. Labrinth
- ★ "Fix You" – Coldplay
- ★ "Warriors" – Imagine Dragons
- ★ "Milkshake" – Kelis
- ★ "Fetish" – Selena Gomez ft. Gucci Mane
- ★ "Wolves" – Selena Gomez, Marshmello
- ★ "Chandelier" – Sia
- ★ "The Greatest" – Sia ft. Kendrick Lamar
- ★ "Boom Pow" – Black Eyed Peas
- ★ "Gold" – Kiiara
- ★ "Aww" – Baby Ariel
- ★ "Perf" – Baby Ariel
- ★ "Candy Cane Lane" – Sia
- ★ "Underneath the Mistletoe" – Sia
- ★ "Snowman" – Sia
- ★ "Ho ho ho" – Sia
- ★ "Centuries" – Fall Out Boy
- ★ "Mr. Saxobeat" – Alexandra Stan
- ★ "My Oh My" – Camila Cabello
- ★ "Believer" – Imagine Dragons
- ★ "Demons" – Imagine Dragons
- ★ "Personal" – HRVY

- ★ "The Less I Know the Better" – Tame Impala
- ★ "Stolen Dance" – Milky Dance
- ★ "Hard Times" – Paramore
- ★ "Photograph" – Ed Sheeran
- ★ "Freak" – Sub Urban ft. REI AMI
- ★ "Cradles" – Sub Urban
- ★ "Boom" – Anjulie
- ★ "Lost in Japan" – Shawn Mendes, Zedd
- ★ "Oceans (Where Feet May Fail)" – Hillsong United
- ★ "Counting Stars" – OneRepublic
- ★ "Why" – Shawn Mendes
- ★ "1-800-273-8755" – Logic ft. Alessia Cara, Khalid
- ★ "I Don't Wanna Live Forever" – Taylor Swift, Zayn
- ★ "Look What You Made Me Do" – Taylor Swift
- ★ "Hurt" – Johnny Cash
- ★ "Creep" – Radiohead
- ★ "Finesse" – Bruno Mars ft. Cardi B
- ★ "Technicolour Beat" – Oh Wonder
- ★ "I Was Made for Loving You" – Kiss
- ★ "Bad at Love" – Halsey
- ★ "I'm an Albatroaz" – Aronchupa
- ★ "Gasoline" - Halsey
- ★ "Rip Her to Shreds" – Boomkat
- ★ "Overdrive" – Katy Rose
- ★ "Operate" – Peaches
- ★ "Rave in the Grave" – Aronchupa, Little Sis Nora
- ★ "God is a DJ" – P!nk
- ★ "Misty Canyon" – Anjali
- ★ "Little Swing" – Aronchupa ft. Little Sis Nora
- ★ "One Way or Another" – Blondie
- ★ "Smoke and Fire" – Sabrina Carpenter
- ★ "Shower" – Becky G
- ★ "Thumbs" – Sabrina Carpenter
- ★ "Eyes Wide Open" – Sabrina Carpenter
- ★ "Me Too" – Meghan Trainor
- ★ "Supernova" – Ansel Elgort
- ★ "A Thousand Years" – Christina Perri
- ★ "Jar of Hearts" – Christina Perri
- ★ "I Don't Know My Name" – Grace VanderWaal
- ★ "Love Is the Name" – Sofia Carson
- ★ "Boombox" – Laura Marano
- ★ "Written in the Stars" – Girl and the Dreamcatcher
- ★ "Day in Paris" – LLusion
- ★ "We Are the Stars" – Sabrina Carpenter

- ★ "Lost Boy" – Ruth B
- ★ "Same Effect" – BENEE
- ★ "My Oh My" – Camila Cabello
- ★ "Most Girls" – Hailey Steinfeld
- ★ "Breath" – Mackenzie Ziegler
- ★ "One of Us" – New Politics
- ★ "American Boy" – Estelle
- ★ "Glitter" – Benee
- ★ "Supalonely" – BENEE ft. Gus Dapperton
- ★ "Me and My Broken Heart" – Rixton
- ★ "Dream On" – Aerosmith
- ★ "Juice" – Lizzo
- ★ "Truth Hurts" – Lizzo
- ★ "Good as Hell" – Lizzo
- ★ "Don't Pass Me By" – The Beatles
- ★ "Yellow Submarine" – The Beatles
- ★ "Help!" – The Beatles
- ★ "Goodbye, Oh" – Ruth B
- ★ "One Day" – Tate McRae
- ★ "Flaming Hot Cheetos" – Clairo
- ★ "Pretty Girl" – Clairo
- ★ "Pumped Up Kicks" – Foster the People
- ★ "Sit Next to Me" – Foster the People
- ★ "Laughing on the Outside" – Bernadette Carroll
- ★ "Patty Cake" – Kodak Black
- ★ "Dusk till Dawn" – Zayn ft. Sia
- ★ "New Rules" – Dua Lipa
- ★ "Heathens" – Twenty One Pilots
- ★ "IDGAF" – Dua Lipa
- ★ "Doubt" – Twenty One Pilots
- ★ "Ride" – Twenty One Pilots
- ★ "Tear in My Heart" – Twenty One Pilots
- ★ "Migraine" – Twenty One Pilots
- ★ "Kitchen Sink" – Twenty One Pilots
- ★ "My Blood" – Twenty One Pilots
- ★ "Put Your Head on My Shoulder" – Paul Anka
- ★ "Young, Dumb, and Broke" – Khalid
- ★ "Blank Space" – Taylor Swift
- ★ Hollaback Girl – Gwen Stefani
- ★ "Rich Girl" – Gwen Stefani
- ★ "Poker Face" – Lady Gaga
- ★ "Applause" – Lady Gaga
- ★ "The Edge of Glory" – Lady Gaga
- ★ "Paparazzi" – Lady Gaga

* "Bad Romance" – Lady Gaga
* "How Long" – Charlie Puth
* "We Don't Talk Anymore" – Charlie Puth ft. Selena Gomez
* "All-Time Low" – Jon Bellion
* "Water Fountain" – Alec Benjamin
* "Issues" – Julia Michaels
* "See You Again" – Wiz Khalifa ft. Charlie Puth
* "Copycat" – Billie Eilish (I love this queen too. An inspiration to me and many others. I want to meet her someday.)
* "Simple Man" – Lynyrd Skynyrd
* "The Twist" – Chubby Checker
* "Free Bird" – Lynyrd Skynyrd
* "My Boy" – Billie Eilish
* "Crazy" – Gnarls Barkeley
* "Delicate" – Taylor Swift
* "You Need to Calm Down" – Taylor Swift
* "Confident" – Demi Lovato
* "Cool for the Summer" – Demi Lovato
* "S.L.U.T." – Bea Miller
* "Bellyache" – Billie Eilish
* "Bored" – Billie Eilish
* "Party Favor" – Billie Eilish
* "Idontwannabeyouanymore" – Billie Eilish
* "When the Party's Over" – Billie Eilish
* "Icy Girl" – Saweetie
* "Ocean Eyes" – Billie Eilish
* "Puppy Dog Eyes" – Ida Laurberg
* "Picnic for Two" – Frank Tapp
* "South of France" – Comme Ça
* "Holiday" – Lil Nas X
* "Black Dress" – CLC
* "Don't Trust Me" – 3OH!3
* "The Scientist" – Coldplay
* "Something Just Like This" – Coldplay, The Chainsmokers
* "Hate Me" – Blue October
* "Sail" – AWOLnation
* "Teenagers" – My Chemical Romance
* "Black Parade" – My Chemical Romance
* "Imagine" – John Lennon
* "House of Gold" – Twenty One Pilots
* "I'm a Mess" – Bebe Rexha
* "Tiptoe through the Tulips" – Tiny Tim
* "New York, New York" – Frank Sinatra
* "Moonlight" – XXXTentacion

- ★ "Pump It" – The Black Eyed Peas
- ★ "Mama Said" – The Shirelles
- ★ "Rumour Has It" – Adele
- ★ "Hello, I Love You" – The Doors
- ★ "Voodoo" – Godsmack
- ★ "Heaven Knows" – The Pretty Reckless
- ★ "Tongue Tied" – Grouplove
- ★ "Aftermath" – Caravan Palace
- ★ "Fly" – Bloodwitch
- ★ "Moral of the Story" – Ashe
- ★ "The Night We Met" – Lord Huron
- ★ "Panic Room" – Au/Ra
- ★ "Opaul" – Freddie Dredd
- ★ "Cha Cha" – Freddie Dredd
- ★ "7 rings" – Ariana Grande
- ★ "You Broke My Heart Again" – Teqkoi
- ★ "Fitzpleasure" – Alt-J
- ★ "First Aid" – Gus Dapperton
- ★ "Miriam" – Norah Jones
- ★ "We Will Rock You" – Why Mona
- ★ "Post Humorous" – Gus Dapperton
- ★ "Teen Romance" – Lil Peep
- ★ "The Story" – Conan Gray
- ★ "Maniac" – Conan Gray
- ★ "Heather" – Conan Gray
- ★ "Dear God" – Sarah McLachlan
- ★ "Livin' La Vida Loca" – Ricky Martin
- ★ "Crazy Train" – Ozzy Osbourne
- ★ "Fancy" – Reba McEntire
- ★ "Season's Greetings" – Linneah (I want to meet them too! This song made me feel powerful after some people made me feel small, and honestly I'd love to thank them for making this funny song.)
- ★ "Guy.exe" – Superfruit
- ★ "It's Up Freestyle" – Lil Keed
- ★ "A.M." – Lonr.
- ★ "Cherry Cola" – Jon Kowada
- ★ "Outlaw" – NEONI
- ★ "E.T." – Katy Perry
- ★ "Bust a Move" – Young MC
- ★ "Happy Pills" – The Weathers
- ★ "Everybody Talks" – Neon Trees
- ★ "Sweater Weather" – The Neighborhood
- ★ "You Know" – Colony House
- ★ "We Fell in Love in October" – Girl in Red

★ "Summertime Sadness" – Lana Del Rey
★ "I Wanna Be Your Girlfriend" – Girl in Red
★ "Dead Girl in the Pool" – Girl in Red
★ "Girls Like Girls" – Hayley Kiyoko
★ "Electric Love" – Børns
★ "Team" – Lorde
★ "Royals" – Lorde
★ "Hey Lover" – The Daughters of Eve
★ "Party in the USA" – Miley Cyrus
★ "Mother's Daughter" – Miley Cyrus
★ "Under Pressure" – Queen, David Bowie
★ "I Hear the Day Has Come" – Matt Maltese
★ "Smarty" – Lana Del Rey
★ "Shutter Island" – Jessie Reyez
★ "Clint Eastwood" – Gorillaz
★ "Feel Good Inc." – Gorillaz
★ "Lemon" – N.E.R.D., Rihanna
★ "223's" – YNW Melly ft. 9lokknine
★ "Tonight You Belong to Me" – Patience and Prudence
★ "The Record Player Song" – Daisy The Great
★ "Bad Reputation" – Joan Jett
★ "Lollipop" – The Chordettes
★ "Que Sera, Sera" – Doris Day
★ "Prom Dress" – Beach Bunny
★ "Prom Dress" – Mxmtoon
★ "Rockin' Robin" – Bobby Day
★ "Mary" – Big Thief
★ "Ruin My Life" – Zara Larsson
★ "Lips Shut" – Nina Chuba
★ "Lush Life" – Zara Larsson
★ "Coke and Mentos" – Salem Ilese
★ "Never Forget You" – Zara Larsson, MNEK
★ "Seasons in the Sun" – Terry Jacks
★ "Bubblegum" – Clairo
★ "Wait a Minute!" – Willow Smith
★ "DNA" – Lia Marie Johnson
★ "House of the Rising Sun" – The Animals
★ "Rock Around the Clock" – Bill Haley
★ "Toxic" – Britney Spears
★ "Pumpkins Scream in the Dead of Night" – Savage Ga$p
★ "Gives You Hell" – The All-American Rejects
★ "Give Us a Little Love" – Fallulah
★ "Suggestions" – Orelia
★ "Stupid Cupid" – Connie Francis

- ★ "Break My Stride" – Matthew Wilder
- ★ "Tap In" – Saweetie
- ★ "It's Oh So Quiet" – bjork
- ★ "Seven Nation Army" – The White Stripes
- ★ "Hypnotic" – Zella Day
- ★ "The Love Club" – Lorde
- ★ "Tennis Court" – Lorde
- ★ "Plain Jane" – A$AP Ferg
- ★ "Genesis" – Grimes
- ★ "On the Regular" – Shamir
- ★ "House Key" – Lolawolf
- ★ "Laffy Taffy" – D4L
- ★ "In My Feelings" – Drake
- ★ "Coming in the Air Tonight" – Phil Collins
- ★ "We're Going to Be Friends" – The White Stripes
- ★ "Got What I Got" – Jason Aldean
- ★ "Dangerous" – Big Data
- ★ "Same Old Love: – Selena Gomez
- ★ "Kill 'Em with Kindness" – Selena Gomez
- ★ "Like a Love Song" – Selena Gomez
- ★ "Mine" – Bazzi
- ★ "Handclap" – Fitz and the Tantrums
- ★ "Immortals" – Fall Out Boy
- ★ "Sofia" – Clairo
- ★ "Rabbit Hole" – Aviva
- ★ "Therefore I Am" – Billie Eilish
- ★ "Hate Me" – Ellie Goulding, Juice Wrld
- ★ "We Are Young" – F.U.N. ft. Janelle Monae
- ★ "Some Nights" – F.U.N.
- ★ "These Boots Were Made for Walkin'" – Nancy Sinatra
- ★ "New Friends" – Maty Noyes
- ★ "Dominic's Interlude" – Halsey, Dominic Fike
- ★ "Cars with the Boom" – L'Trimm
- ★ "Alanis' Interlude" – Halsey, Alanis Morisette
- ★ "Hey Little Girl" – sophiemarie.b
- ★ "Friends" – Marshmello, Anne-Marie
- ★ "pov" – Ariana Grande
- ★ "Vance Joy" – Riptide
- ★ "Everytime" – boy pablo
- ★ "Sweater Weather" – The Neighborhood
- ★ "If You Could Read My Mind" – Gordon Lightfoot
- ★ "Sweet Dreams" – The Eurythmics
- ★ "Kryptonite" – 3 Doors Down
- ★ "Positions" – Ariana Grande

- ★ **"Watermelon Sugar" – Harry Styles**
- ★ **"I'm Just Snacking" – Gus Dapperton**
- ★ **"Smells Like Teen Spirit" – Nirvana**
- ★ **"Fill Me Up Anthem" – Gus Dapperton**
- ★ **"Kerosene" – Rachel Lorin**
- ★ **"Winter" – BENEE ft. Mallrat**
- ★ **"My Favorite Fish" – Gus Dapperton**
- ★ **"Coax and Botany" – Gus Dapperton**
- ★ **"Prune, You Look Funny" – Gus Dapperton**
- ★ **"Nightmare" – Halsey**
- ★ **"Mickey" – Toni Basil**

Here are some quotes that helped inspire me:

"If you ever say never too late, I'll forget the diamonds you ate." – My Chemical Romance, "To the End"

"In the middle of a gunfight. In the center of a restaurant. They say, come with your arms raised high. Well, they're never gonna get me. And like a bullet through a flock of doves." – My Chemical Romance, "You Know What They Do to Guys Like Us in Prison"

"I don't think the world is sold on just doing what we're told." – OneRepublic, "Counting Stars"

"It's the way it is, you know. Everything must come to an end, the drip finally stops." – Herb Kazzazz from "Bojack Horseman"

"We love our bread, we love our butter, but most of all, we love each other." – *Madeline*

"We are the weirdos, mister." – Nancy Downs from *The Craft*

"Jealous? You don't even exist to me." – Nancy Downs from *The Craft*

"People fear what they don't understand and hate what they can't conquer." – Andrew Smith

"Will happen, happening, happened." – *Adventure Time*

For all of you readers out there, look up from your book once in a while and maybe you will find that you don't need a book to find magic or happiness. Sometimes it's right there in front of you. And for those who wish to find some magic, step outside and study the scenery; it will hopefully be your guide to find your own sort of magic. I want all of you to be happy and healthy in your lives. Don't use my book as an escape but as a tool. Use it to show that your life is so magical although you might not see it yet. There are close to eight billion people on this planet, and we all live a different day every day. I don't know about you, but I think that's pretty darn special. You are so important, and the world would not be the way it is without you. How special is it to think that every action you have ever made changed the course of the world? I love all of you!

And for all those people who are told that they are too young, too illiterate, that you don't meet the qualifications, you are valid and important. You can do great things when you listen to yourself instead of the negative views society spews out and onto you. Also, NEVER let someone censor your world. The more we censor our reading, music, television, etc., the more we don't get the authentic version. We all deserve to know the real, true version of everything. Happy reading, my loves! Muah. ~ WH

CHAPTER 1

➤ ➤

MEHREEN KENNA

"Rhyann! Seraphina! Mehreen! Get out of that nasty ditch! What on earth are you doing?" called our mother, Salem. Admittedly, I was only giving half of my attention because my mind is always preoccupied with nonsensical questions. My brain feels flooded all the time. I wish someone would turn off the ever-running spigot that is my mind. A couple twists and ah—no more me. I could be a silent watcher in the room and nobody would have to hear the goings-on of my thoughts anymore. Or maybe I'll wait for winter and the spigot that is my brain will freeze in an overnight haste. No such luck would come to me, however. No such luck.

Yesterday my mind ran circles around the hope of a world without fear of death or loss. However, as long as the world has humans inhabiting it, those things will never cease to exist. Today posed a new question: What if the imaginary friends we made up as children were people we were supposed to meet but died before we had the chance? As depressing as it might sound, it gave me something to think about. Something other than the sinking ship that is my life. Every day I feel as if I am reliving the same experiences. Nothing changes, nothing ever becomes better.

I heard the screen door shut as my dad, Alan, came outside. He and my mom are very different. My mom—with all her insecurities—projects every little thing on me because Rhyann and Seraphina are her little miracle babies, whilst my dad loves all three of us the same. She shames me for going days without shaving or leaving my hair down instead of putting it into a ponytail like a "proper young lady." My dad, however, always kisses me on the cheek and says the same lie over and over: That I am beautiful. I always wonder if he'll leave my mom. She started bullying me after Rhyann and Seraphina were born, but sadly, as I have come to find out, his love for my mom is stronger than his fatherly love for me. Maybe he believes that if he leaves, she'll take Rhyann and Seraphina with her.

My dad just came home from work, with his hair imbued with gel into a slick style, in his flannel and with a brown belt tightened around his pants. He looked so professional, and I wished that I could be as professional and successful as him someday. I want to be the rich man that my mom wants me to marry. I'll be damned if I let a man determine my worth. Or woman, as a matter of fact. My mom believes that I will never amount to anything. After hearing the same negative thing and having it drilled into my head constantly, I am coming to believe that what she says is true.

My mom waves her hand over my face and says, "Mehreen Kenna! Hey, what is going on? I have been calling your name for ten minutes! Do I need to schedule an appointment with an otolaryngologist? Because it seems like your ears need to be checked." She went on and on and on. And the longer she talked, the more I drowned her out with my own thoughts. I walked up to the porch where my dad was waiting with Rhyann and Seraphina. My dad wrapped a thick, fresh-smelling towel around each one of us.

I debated whether I should listen to my mom's rant or blow her off and go inside. The latter seems to be the best option for me, but the former would get me out of a rant later on. "Mehreen, you are seventeen years old. You are going to graduate in four days! Four! You were in charge of Rhyann and Seraphina while we were gone, and I come home to all three of you splish-splashing the ditch? Really?"

A single tear streamed down my cheek and tickled my face. I responded, "Mom, Rhyann and Seraphina are seven and eight years old! They aren't babies anymore! They can take care of themselves. I thought it would be fun for them if we caught some frogs and just enjoyed nature for once. I am going to be so glad when I graduate because I can leave this house and never look back. I am not appreciated or seen here. I am not even sure why I am arguing with you. You don't have the capacity to think about anyone else's view but your own."

My mom turned her angered, dour expression into a confused, almost hurt look. She was visibly stunned. Rhyann and Seraphina screeched in unison, "Don't go, Mehreen!" I looked over to see how my dad would react. His response was the one that mattered most to me. Was he going to side with Mom and chastise me for yelling at her? Or was he going to be on my side and agree that Mom is too hard on me? He looked conflicted as if he couldn't decide which one of us to choose. My dad didn't say a word and looked downward as if he was ashamed of himself. I can guess what he was ashamed of. Ashamed that the woman he fell in love with has changed and, although he loves his kids, he doesn't have the vagina to leave her. That's right, you heard me. Why say balls when clearly they are the weaker genitalia? One swift kick to the balls and you're down. If you have a vagina, however, you can push a whole child through and withstand a massive amount of pain. He still believes that somewhere deep down, that woman he fell in love with is still there.

Angered at my dad and my mom, I trudged into my room, tears streaming down my face. I flopped on my bed and shrugged as I remembered that I was soaked in ditch water. My bed needed new sheets anyway. I sat up from the bed and sauntered into my bathroom, its clear tiles creaking under my green-painted toenails. I slid off my clothes and thought of a saying from my childhood. Whenever my grandma would bathe me, she would slip off my shirt over my head and say, "There's more than one way to skin a cat." I miss her dearly. She would have never let my mom treat me this way.

I stepped into my bathtub. I sat down and got a damp, chilly feeling. Has somebody recently taken a bath or shower in my bathroom besides me? I hadn't had a shower for at least a day and a half. If I were a betting kind of person, I'd put my money on either Rhyann or Seraphina. My mom would never come into my room. She thinks I'm a slob and that if she came into my room, she'll contract a disease. No joke, either; that is something she actually said to my face before. As for my dad, after work he is either playing with Rhyann and Seraphina and talking to my mom, or in his self-proclaimed "man cave," which is basically just our fruit cellar with cable and pizza pockets.

I started filling the bath with the most scalding water I could find, and I inserted a washcloth as a plug to keep the water from draining. As I always say, have the water feel like molten lava, or go home. I lay back in the bath, my head just above the water so that I did not drown. My hair flowed, and it felt like damp yarn on my back as I stared up at the ceiling, gazing at nothing. I daydreamed of an imaginary friend. I named her Khaleesi, the name of my best friend who left school three weeks into seventh grade. She's as good as imaginary now.

As I envisioned my imaginary friend, I made her features just the same as Khaleesi's—deep, entrancing blue eyes, turquoise cat-eye glasses, twenty inches of surfer-blonde hair that is always tied back with her bedazzled, hazel-colored scrunchie that wraps her hair in a low ponytail. She had copper skin with speckles of twinkling white from her shimmer mist body spray. Her favorite outfit was a pair of black basketball shorts and a violet long sleeve that said an inspirational quote. She always had the scent of tangerines and raisins surrounding her. I miss her dearly.

Khaleesi and I used to go outside my house and pick a tree to sit under. We would drink the sourest lemonade we could find and talk about our home lives. Khaleesi didn't have the greatest time at home, so she spent most of her time with me at mine. I still cannot believe I haven't seen her since seventh grade. That feels like a lifetime and a half ago.

In seventh grade, Khaleesi's mom, Freya, worked at a bank that has since closed down. One day Freya had been caught stealing money from different clients' bank accounts, and the police were after her. It wasn't the first time she had done something like that. I remember the day they caught Freya. She was sentenced fifteen years for robbing the bank and aggravated assault. After the trial, a social worker took Khaleesi and put her into foster care. I cried and cried that day. I haven't seen her or heard from her since.

I felt so empty, bare, and numb for so long. It is crazy to think that she's a distant memory now. What has become of her? The question rings in my head like a small town's church bell. I hope she does momentous things in her lifetime. I am horrified at the thought of her becoming like Freya; luckily, she's anything but.

The bathwater was starting to become ice cold. I sat up and took the washcloth out of the drain. I watched all the water swirl down until there was nothing left. I stood up and turned the showerhead on. I cracked open a bottle of shampoo, and ran my fingers through my hair. I washed and washed until the smell of ditch water was no longer there. I squirted a quarter-sized amount of cream rinse in my hand and washed that through my hair too.

I grabbed my bottle of blackberry body gel and scrubbed and scrubbed and scrubbed until my body was left with no ditch stench. Finally, I toweled off and grabbed some comfy bed clothes. I leisurely put on a pair of silky, purple shorts and an old-lady nightgown. It had a light blue floral print. I "borrowed" it from my mom. What could possibly go wrong?

I braided my bone-white hair into a Dutch style and tied it back with a white, sparkly hair tie. I walked over to my bed and took all the sheets off. I bunched all of the sheets into a small bundle and took them to the laundry room. I saw that my mom had started a load of clothes already, so I left my sheets in the laundry bin. I cannot wait for that lecture.

I sashayed back to my room, feeling great about myself because I stood up to my mom. I feel on top of the world right now. I sat down on my mint green, comfy stool. I saw that my lipsticks were scattered in front of my vanity mirror, and I decided to clean this unholy mess. I sorted them by color: purple had fig, coneflower, eggplant, boysenberry. Next was red: merlot, garnet, blush. The pink supply was endless: taffy, fuchsia, ballet slipper, cerise, flamingo, magenta, salmon, watermelon, bubblegum. I only had ultramarine and baby blue in my blue section, so I moved onto tan. Tan consisted of biscotti, mocha, oyster, and sandcastle. They were all so very different but the same in a weird way. I had the most lipsticks in the color green: crocodile, pistachio, juniper, shamrock, viridian, chartreuse, green apple, forest green, kale, key lime, pea soup, seaweed, and kelp.

Mom bought the most makeup for me out of the three daughters she has. You might be thinking that it's her small way of showing that she loves me, but you are dead wrong. She buys me the most makeup because she thinks I need it the most, that I need to cover up my features. Maybe she thinks that with all this makeup, I can paint myself into a version that she can love. I haven't been the most successful painter, as you would have already guessed.

Beauty has always boggled my mind. It is supposed to be a thing of the heart, not the body. However, they say this is a man's world, and a woman's job is to be pretty. If it were mine, I'd be fired within the hour. I have never cared about what I looked like. I never wanted to succumb to patriarchal ideologies. The skin we live in is just temporary. It doesn't define us as a person. When I die, nobody is going to come to my funeral and say, "She had a nice ass. I'm going to miss her six-pack so bad." They are going to talk about what I did in life, the kindness I spread.

I wish my mom knew how toxic her beliefs were. It has Rhyann and Seraphina smearing makeup on their faces daily, thinking that they need a prince to come and sweep them off their feet. Well, guess what? Prince Charming needed a shoe to find Cinderella because he couldn't recognize her without makeup! If that doesn't give you some sort of idea of how messed up society's idea of beauty is then I don't know what else to say. Girls don't need princes to come save them. Girls need to be their own "prince" and save themselves. The only way they can be truly loved is if they love themselves first.

My Aunt Kehlani and cousins, Zahra and Jaimini, used to enter themselves into beauty contests. They wouldn't put a dab of makeup on their faces nor would they dress up. Their hair would be in knots, and their shoes would be dirty. People would ask them why they even bother entering the contest if they "weren't going to put any effort in." My Aunt Kehlani would always respond, "Beauty shouldn't take any effort. Compassion, empathy, kindness, love—those are the amalgamation of beauty. If you love makeup, and that's what makes you feel like yourself, then that's incredible; have fun. However, if you use makeup because you think it's your duty to dress up, to be perfect, and to be used as a tool to please people, then you are in error. You are beautiful not because of what you look like on the outside but because of the love and warmth you radiate."

Aunt Kehlani asked me quite a few times if I wanted to go with her, Zahra, and Jaimini to advocate against toxic beauty standards. Each time I wanted to go with my whole heart, but my mom thought that the idea of it was ridiculous, so I was never allowed to go. Sometimes I wonder how Aunt Kehlani and my mother grew up in the same house but turned out so drastically different.

I basked in the fruity, powdery scent of my freshly-applied deodorant. I picked up my bleach-smelling, yellow-paged thought journal. My question was bugging me, daring me to write about it.

Question of the day: What if imaginary friends were supposed to be people you met but died before you could?

Khaleesi and Freya were in my life for a long time. When I was five to six years old, the same as Khaleesi, I didn't have anyone to play with. That was before Khaleesi had the strength to fight back against Freya's abuse. During that time, to cope with everything horrible going on, I made up an imaginary friend named Hynlie.

4

Hynlie was serendipitous and had wonderful parents. She always invited me to sleepovers with feather pillows and comfy bean bags. I even made up other imaginary friends that Hynlie was friends with: Shoogam, Xia, Rosalinde, and Glishia were their names. It was all fun and games until I got my kind of slap-in-the-face reality check of Khaleesi coming to cry on my shoulder.

Khaleesi was a fast bruiser; she'd always come to me with purple blemishes the size of the baseballs Freya threw at her. One day when we were six years old, Khaleesi came to my house. She had all sorts of cigar burns on her wrists. I was so done with Freya's bullshit. Khaleesi lay in bed with me as I rubbed her back. My mom called the police as she usually did when we found Khaleesi bruised and battered. Unfortunately, it was the same result over and over. They wouldn't do anything about it.

That night, Khaleesi cried herself to sleep in my arms. I decided that I had to do something. I sneakily crawled out of my bed, making sure Khaleesi was comfortable. I cracked open my window and crawled through it with precision. I closed the window so that my mom wouldn't suspect anything and Khaleesi wouldn't realize what I was doing and chase after me.

I sprinted the two-mile trip to Freya's house, and I didn't make a single peep. I knew Freya didn't lock her door because she refused to pay for a replacement key. She threw the old key in a pond when she found out she was pregnant with Khaleesi. The house was pitch-black, and I decided then that it was now or never. I turned the doorknob gently so that it wouldn't creak, and I tiptoed into the doorway.

Freya appeared to be drowsy; she was draped over the couch like a rag doll, a foreign alcoholic drink in one hand. Freya's other hand held a cigar with some smoke swirling around it. Freya muttered, "Khaleesi, why are you such a waste of space? Make yourself useful and get my lighter, would you?" It was dark and she was very drunk, so she mistook me for Khaleesi. Exactly what I wanted to happen.

I needed Freya to think that I was Khaleesi so that if I got beaten, I could call the cops after she passed out. I had already planned what I was going to say back and forth with the policeman. I know now, looking back, that my plan sounds bad especially after the cops wouldn't do anything before. I could've been killed. I knew that then, just as well as I do now. I didn't care. I wanted Khaleesi to have some sort of justice in her life.

I was going to tell the cops that I had been kidnapped by Freya while having a sleepover with Khaleesi at my house. Sure, I would have to tell a lie, but it was worth it if it meant helping out my best friend. I asked Freya in my best Khaleesi voice, "Ma'am, I am exhausted, and I have no idea where your lighter is." I kicked myself inside. Khaleesi would never say anything of the sort. She always obeyed and figured it out. I hoped that Freya wouldn't figure out it was me.

I knew that what I said angered Freya, especially since I said it in a calm, cheery voice. Freya loved undying misery because she herself was miserable. She felt that hurting other people made her strong. However, it only showed how weak she was.

"Excuse me? Am I so old as to be called ma'am? Get your lazy ass over here and look me in the eye! You are to address me as 'queen.' I am your ruler, and you will obey me!" I watched my steps across the messy floor and got really close to her face. She still thought I was Khaleesi. She took her bottle and slammed it down on my exposed feet. I was in utter agony as I watched the crimson color of blood spread across my feet.

I had to suppress the urge to scream and cry. Khaleesi never cried in front of Freya. She always waited until she got to my house to let it all out. She didn't want to seem weak. The weaker you seemed, the more powerful and violent Freya became.

After a few seconds had gone by, Freya slapped me across the face. It stung worse than ten bee stings. Freya demanded, "Now, go get my lighter for me. Look in the cabinet drawer." The cabinet was right next to her; it just proved yet again how heinous she was. I handed the lighter to her. I left the room with Freya grimacing, and I found Khaleesi's home phone. Before I dialed anything, I sat back and thanked all the heavens

5

and stars that I had my parents. That they took care of me. Well, before Rhyann and Seraphina were born three and four years later.

To think a mother could do that to her own child made my heart shatter into a million pieces. She didn't even recognize that I wasn't Khaleesi. It made me question so many things. I cowardly hid under the coffee table in the kitchen and dialed 911. I had the same conversation with the police as I had imagined, and Freya was arrested. Khaleesi stayed with us for a while. I remember eavesdropping on my parents' hushed conversations and hearing them say that the police only believed me because I had white privilege. Khaleesi was a person of color. It was a concept I didn't understand until much later on.

Four months later, Freya was let out on some sort of technicality. Khaleesi had to go back to that mess. The only reason we couldn't foster Khaleesi when we were in seventh grade was because the social workers were afraid that Freya would get out and try to harm Khaleesi. So, they had to take her away. Far away.

That night, after Freya was arrested for hurting me, Khaleesi hugged me as tight as a boa constrictor around its prey. She kissed my cheek and thanked me for releasing her from the hell she was in. Well, not in those exact words. We were six. Wow, that sentence truly hit me like a brick. We were six. SIX! And we had already gone through so much. After I explained to my mom what I had done, instead of being angry and lashing out, she wailed, "Oh, baby. Good Lord. Freya can't hurt you here. Baby, it's okay." It was a phrase that my mom always used to try and calm Khaleesi down. My mom hugged me for so long, I didn't think she'd ever let go.

Sometimes I battled in my mind whether my life would've been better if Hynlie was real and Khaleesi was imaginary. I think it's true that imaginary friends are people we're supposed to meet, but I would much rather have Khaleesi. Hynlie would've been the commercial-like, American Girl Doll kind of friend. She would have been perfect. Khaleesi was far from perfect, and she taught me so many things while being so young. I had to grow up fast, but it contributed to the woman I am becoming now.

If I truly think about it, if I lived in an alternate universe where Khaleesi wasn't born and Hynlie was real, I'd be the Khaleesi in the situation. And Hynlie would be my Mehreen. Instead of being the one who saved others, I would be getting saved. The roles would be flip-flopped. Maybe the life you've always dreamt of died out so that this lesson-filled life we have could teach us. Hmm . . .

Until next time,
Mehreen Kenna

I finished writing and decided to do my homework for Mr. Alender and Ms. Boie. I'm not a take-my-book-to-lunch nerd, but I don't have the IQ of a bottle of nail polish either. I'm somewhere in between those two drastic choices. I can be book smart and feel really confident about my grades and everything. However, on some days I find myself checking five plus five on a calculator. I wonder what that says about me.

As for Rhyann and Seraphina, they barely pass each grade. Mom mollycoddles them to a point where I want to tear out my own hair. Sometimes I get the nagging thought at the back of my brain that maybe Mom cossets them so much because she doesn't want them to go through anything like what I had to go through. It makes perfect sense, but it doesn't give my mom any right to discard me like an old can of tuna.

I spent my last four days of high school like usual, and I felt more excitement as each day passed. Soon, I was going to be free of this place and my family. On the last day, I looked at my locker and traced my finger around the combination dial. I remember the first day of my freshman year. I yearned for Khaleesi to be there, to be able to walk down the hallway with her, our eyes bright and hopeful for the next four years. Well, I didn't get Khaleesi, and I sure as hell didn't get the high school life I had pictured for myself. Full disclosure, *High School Musical* is an inaccurate description of what high school is like.

Graduation day was a total blur. I spent the whole morning looking at myself in the mirror with my cap and gown on. It felt surreal to finally be done. I sat on my bed and looked at my college brochure. *Go Blue Devils! Community college, here I come!* Just another reason for my mom to despise me. I didn't want to apply for any big league schools because I didn't want the financial debt following me around my whole life. Community college would get me a degree and was more financially suitable for me. However, my mom didn't see it that way. But hey, when did she ever agree with me?

Mom dressed in a flowy, white dress and black penny loafers. She pinned her hair up very neatly and applied her makeup heavily. My dad wore a nice suit that matched my mom's dress, and Rhyann and Seraphina wore matching dresses. Their dresses were tan with a black belt, and they had tan tennis shoes on. Under my cap and gown, I wore a tight, lacy, dark green dress and white high heels. I left my hair down, and I used a curling iron to make my hair wavy and presentable. *Oh, Lord. Please slap me! I said presentable. I am truly starting to sound like my mother.*

My mom came into my room and shut the door behind her. She sat on the bed next to me and did something that I didn't expect her to. It was something she hadn't really done in quite some time. She hugged me. She hugged me as tight as the night I pretended to be Khaleesi to get Freya arrested. I hugged her back, and she started sobbing very quietly, her body starting to shake. After about ten minutes, she released me from her arms and looked at me. I rubbed her back and asked calmly, "Mom, is everything okay?"

"Mehreen Fern Kenna, you are my firstborn. I cannot believe my baby is graduating today. You mean more to me than you will ever realize. I know that things have changed since Rhyanna and Seraphina were born. I know that I have been a shitty mother to you. I am eternally sorry. I thought by babying them and protecting them they wouldn't have to go through what you had to growing up. But I got so carried away with protecting them that I forgot to protect you. I thought I was being hard on you as a way to show that I love and care for you, but that was just a lie I told myself. I realize now that all the things I have said were hateful and I was bullying my own daughter. I was *bullying* you! I am so sorry."

My mom got off the bed and grabbed a tissue. She sat back on the bed and cried and cried. I tried to hold back my tears; it was almost too much to bear. She continued, "I need you to know that I think you are beautiful and smart; you are the amalgamation of everything I could have ever wished to have in a daughter. I said all those hateful things because I needed somebody to project my anger onto. I have been in deep depression for years, and you are the first person I have told about it. I know it isn't fair. It isn't right. It doesn't excuse my behavior. I will forever be trying to make it up to you. I know I can never truly make up for everything. I hope you can forgive me." She blew her nose into the tissue.

My thoughts were racing a thousand miles a minute. I wasn't sure what to say. The only thing that I knew was that I forgave her. I wanted my mom back. That's what I have always wanted. "Mom, of course I forgive you. For so many years I thought you hated me. I thought that I didn't even exist to you anymore after Rhyann and Seraphina were born. I am so sorry that you had to battle this alone. I am so, so sorry. I wish I had been there for you from the start. Why didn't you tell anybody? Why didn't you tell dad at least? We could've helped you!"

"Mehreen, you need to brace yourself for what I am about to tell you," she warned. I told her that I was ready for whatever she was about to tell me. She explained, "Ever since Khaleesi was taken away by that social worker when you girls were in seventh grade, I haven't been the same. It changed me as I am sure it changed you. That night I contacted the social worker who had Khaleesi, and I asked her to update me about Khaleesi once a week. I didn't tell your father because I knew he would tell you. I didn't want you to know anything about it because I knew you'd want her here. But we had to keep her far away so that Freya could never hurt that poor child ever again. I just wanted to know that Khaleesi would be okay."

Mom paused for a second, and I asked in a confused tone, "Mom, that's more than understandable. If I knew you were getting updates about her, I'd probably scream until my face was red for you to bring her here. Why would I need to brace myself for something as simple as that?"

Mom answered, "You didn't let me finish. All the calls had been pretty good; she was adjusting to her foster family. She missed you terribly, but she was doing well for the most part. She was safe, and that's what mattered. However, three months later I got a call that I will never forget." My mom held my hands in her hands and looked into my eyes.

"Baby, the social worker called, and she said that there was a house fire and Khaleesi was in it. It was an accident. Her foster mom had left the oven burner on in the kitchen and forgot to turn it off before everybody went to bed. Khaleesi didn't make it out."

I felt sick to my stomach. I vomited on my bed, and I started sobbing crocodile tears. My heart felt like it had been shattered into a million pieces.

I had always known that I probably wouldn't see Khaleesi again, but the thought of her having a long, happy life kept me sane for the longest time. But to think that she had been gone for almost five years and I didn't know anything about it? It made my insides burst into flames with the burning rage I was feeling. I screamed at the top of my lungs. I sounded like a banshee, but I didn't care. My mom grabbed me and pulled me close to her. "Mehreen, baby, I am so sorry. This secret has been eating away at me for years. I never wanted to tell you because I knew it would absolutely break your heart. But it's been gnawing at me for so long, and I needed you to know the truth. Please don't think any less of me."

I didn't think any less of her, to be truthful. Carrying that heavy burden alone took strength. She knew that news like that would utterly destroy me. I had already been through so much already, and she didn't want to put me through any more. I cannot imagine what my mom must've gone through. She must be blaming herself for Khaleesi's untimely death. If we just fought to keep her with us, she would've grown up. She would've lived.

"Mom, I love you. I understand why you did what you did. You were protecting me from a world of grief. I am truly grateful, but I never want you to go through something like that alone. Family is first. It *has* to be like that. We are all here for you. You matter. I want you in my life, happy and thriving," I said through sniffles and hushed crying.

"Mehreen, I love you to the moon and way beyond the stars," my mom said to me, right before planting a kiss on my cheek. I started taking deep breaths after I finished crying. I just cannot believe my childhood best friend was gone. My mom got up from the bed and stood in front of my vanity mirror.

"Mehreen, I know I have put you through more than I could ever make up for. For example, I know you hate makeup and shaving because you are comfortable in your own skin, and you wanna show off how naturally beautiful you are. You don't want to succumb to societal beauty standards. I was jealous of you for a long time. I was also jealous of Kehlani, Zahra, and Jaimini. You four have so much self-love, and when I look at myself, all I see is ugliness and self-loathing. So I took my own insecurities and spewed them onto you. And in my opinion, that's one of the most heinous things I could have ever done. You are so beautiful. In fact, your beauty is ethereal. Mehreen, you don't need any of this makeup. I am so sorry that I ever pushed all of this garbage on you and your sisters."

My mom picked up a bottle of lip gloss and threw it in my trash can. Then, she grabbed some of my eyeshadow palettes and threw them in the trash can too. She grabbed a tube of mascara, and I stopped her before she threw it away. I told her about some nifty organization that uses the brushes from mascara tubes to clean oil and other stuff off of wildlife. So we kept those but threw EVERYTHING else away. It felt so empowering. Minutes later, Rhyann and Seraphina opened the door and came in.

Rhyann asked, "Is everything okay? Seraphina and I heard screaming and crying. Daddy said that it was okay and we should stay out, but we wanted to check on you."

Seraphina said, "Mehreen, is Mom being nice to you? We don't want you to leave." Rhyann and Seraphina came and gave me some hugs.

I answered, "Mom loves me, and we understand each other better now. I am never leaving you girls." I saw something out of the corner of my eye and realized that my dad was standing in the doorway, listening.

I waved to my dad to come over, and he joined us. All five of us stood together in a long hug, and it felt nice to finally be a family again. Together as one. Finally, we all got our things gathered up and piled in the car. Dad drove us to the school. Before I went with my classmates, Dad pulled me aside. "Mehreen, you are everything I wanted in a daughter and more. I am so proud of you." He started crying and kissed me on the forehead. He quickly wiped away his tears before Rhyann and Seraphina could see. "Now go, show them that the Kennas know how to graduate!" I hugged him and walked into the high school.

I walked into the gym where teachers had already started seating people alphabetically. I was crammed in between Silas Karne and Bryleigh Kitzmiller. Silas wasn't going to be graduating because he needed to make up some classes in the summer. I guess he just wanted to sit with us. As I sat there, watching everybody talk nervously about their futures, cry about leaving, etc., I looked around and was amazed. The kids I have known since I was a little kid seemed all grown up. That meant I had grown up too. We were all going to be adults soon, which boggled my mind beyond comprehension. We weren't kids anymore.

The ceremony started, and speeches were made. When Principal Middleton announced, "Mehreen Fern Kenna," I froze in place.

Bryleigh gently tapped me on the shoulder and said, "Reen, go get your diploma. You've earned it. You've made it, babe."

I walked up to Principal Middleton and accepted my diploma. I shook her hand and walked back to my seat. I could hear my mom, Dad, Rhyann, and Seraphina cheering for me. I felt so accomplished.

After they had announced all of our names, they let the valedictorians give their speeches. Principal Middleton announced, "The valedictorians of this graduating class are Zuri Adamson, Yazminn Beneet, Breagha Hicks, Pari Jack, and Maibelle Yerry." As they walked up to the stage, everybody clapped, including me. Everybody except Silas. He whispered in my ear, "They've been honor roll students since they got out of the womb. The only person they've probably ever had a crush on is Mickey Mouse."

I think Silas thought he was being hilarious by making fun of them, but I knew just what to say to put him in his place. "Let me make a joke, Silas. How does a misogynistic asshole with straight Fs graduate high school? Oh, wait, I guess we'll never know." He looked stunned. I wasn't going to let him put those girls down. They have worked way too hard to be put down. They are strong and wonderful. Hell, Breagha will probably be my doctor someday, and Pari, the president. All of those girls will go so far in life, it's crazy.

After each of them gave speeches, we were dismissed. We had a small party back at my house, with just Mom, Dad, Rhyann, Seraphina, and me. We spent the night looking through old photo albums, eating cheesy pizza, and watching corny, B-rated horror movies. It was a perfect end to an amazing day. After we finished the fifth horror movie, I looked over and saw I was the only one who was still awake. I got up from the couch and covered them with a quilt. I scampered off to bed, smiling from ear to ear.

When I woke up in the morning, I put on the song "Happy" by Pharrell Williams as I brushed my teeth and danced with utter glee. Well, I probably should not have danced with a toothbrush in my mouth, but that is beside the point. I put on my favorite shirt and shorts, and slipped on a pair of comfy moccasins. I walked out the door, and saw Rhyann and Seraphina in their dance clothes.

"You two look very spiffy," I complimented. They ran up to me and gave me a squeeze.

"Mehreen, can you please take us to dance class today?" Seraphina asked while giving me puppy-dog eyes.

"Yes, of course I will! Get your shoes on, and I'll meet you downstairs," I told them.

They giggled in unison and ran downstairs. I ran my fingers through my hair and grabbed my purse and keys. I walked down the stairs and into the kitchen. Mom and Dad were at the kitchen table, drinking coffee and talking about the newspaper. They thanked me for taking Rhyann and Seraphina to dance class. I gave each of them a hug and a kiss, and told them that I loved them and that I would be back soon.

I looked at the door. Rhyann and Seraphina were already standing beside my car. They looked so graceful in their little outfits. I had spent so long resenting them because I thought my mom loved them more. Now that I know the whole truth, I am so proud to be their sister. We all hopped in the car and buckled ourselves in. I put my key into the ignition and looked at my side mirror. I turned on some happy, upbeat music, and we were all singing the lyrics. We had no care in the world. I was driving down the road when suddenly, I saw a light blue pickup truck swerving in and out of the lanes in front of me. I slowed down and backed up so that I wouldn't come in contact with that dill weed. However, I didn't back up fast enough. I looked back to see Rhyann and Seraphina screaming and holding each other. I saw an Audi pull out of a driveway near us, and I looked back in front of me. *Crash.* I saw the light as bright as ever.

CHAPTER 2

KIELY COSMOSIS

I pulled out of my driveway, and I watched a blue pickup truck plow into a small car with a female driver. She seemed to be my age or so. I didn't fully process what was happening until minutes after the damage was already done. The whole car had been flipped over. I backed my car up in my driveway and ran up to the car. I opened the door and pulled the driver out. I found her driver's license; it said her name was Mehreen Kenna. I checked for a pulse and couldn't find one. She was gone. I noticed that there were two little girls in the backseat.

I pried open the door to the backseat. I checked each of them for a pulse, and they had passed away too. I dialed 911 and told them everything. As I was talking to them, I walked up to the blue pickup truck and found a middle-aged woman with more needles in her arm than I could count on my two hands. Soon, the police and ambulances arrived, and they said they would take care of everything else.

I walked back up to my car and drove away. I placed one hand on my steering wheel and one hand on my stomach. I felt so sickened by what I had just seen. How could someone be that selfish as to kill three innocent girls? They had years of life left in them, but all of that went down the drain the second that woman hit them. People like that woman make me want to scream in rage.

My stomach hurt out of grief for those girls, but that's not the only reason it hurt. There was an immense amount of nervousness swelling up inside of me. I had a fight with my mom, Jyoti, and my dad, Petey, this morning. They had threatened to kick me out months ago if I wasn't accepted into a college. They didn't want me going to community college because "Cosmosises went to Ivy League schools." I was a failure in their eyes.

After our fight this morning, I packed all of my earthly possessions into boxes, and I stuffed them in my car. Mckai and Annyn, my younger sisters, found out what had happened, and they screamed bloody murder until my parents told them, "Fine. Go with Kiely! You won't last a week!" So, we had to put the little bit of belongings they had into my car too. I didn't have much money, and I never planned for them to come with me. I had no idea what I was going to do. Then, I pulled out of my driveway just in time to see the untimely deaths of three girls. I didn't know what the universe was trying to tell me. I was lost in this world, without anyone coming to find me. I was that treasure box that no one could find, but when they do, nothing is inside.

"Kiely, Annyn, and I are hungry. Please try to get us something to eat," said Mckai.

I felt bad for my sisters, but it's not like I made them come. As I had said before, I didn't have much cash; it was barely enough to pay for lunch. I pulled into a drive-thru at McDonald's and pulled out my wallet with Sesame Street characters on it.

"Hello, welcome to McDonald's! My name is Sutton, I will be taking your order today," said a woman in a very cheerful tone from the speaker.

I looked behind me and asked what they wanted to order. After they answered, I cleared my throat and said to the speaker, "I would like a ten-piece chicken nugget with honey mustard; one spicy chicken sandwich with lettuce, tomato, and mayonnaise; and two small Mountain Dews." The speaker told me the total price, and I pulled up to the second window to pay. Another car was in front of me, so I had to wait a couple minutes.

Annyn said, "Kiely, what are you going to eat?"

To be honest, I had no clue. I had spent what little money I had on this meal. Why did my parents have to punish me even more? They knew that Mckai and Annyn would be another task for me to deal with. I adore my sisters just as much as they adore me, but I know I am way underqualified to take care of them. I wish they just stayed with my parents. The car in front of me pulled away with all of their purchases, and I pulled up to the next window. I inhaled the salty smell and sighed. A lady in her thirties handed me a greasy paper bag, and I handed it to Mckai and Annyn in the back.

I pulled the money out of my wallet and handed it to the cashier. Her eyes seemed to light up as she gave me a toothy smile. She had fiery red hair that framed her face and bright, pink glasses. She grabbed my receipt and gave it to me. I crinkled my receipt and put it in my wallet. Just as I was about to pull out of the drive-thru, the cashier said, "I know this is very unprofessional and could result in me getting fired for asking, but are you okay? You seem like you've been crying. Please forgive me for being nosy, but I try to make sure that everyone I come into contact with leaves happily whether they came to me that way or not."

I replied, "Well, I have been through the wringer today, my sisters included. I appreciate your thoughtfulness, but I don't think there's much you could do for our current situation."

The cashier responded, "Something can always be done. Would you like to come inside?"

I didn't know how to feel about her. She seemed kind and understanding, but I had just met her not even ten minutes ago. How was I supposed to trust her? What did she have to gain by helping me? I decided that I needed any help I could get, so I told her that I would be inside soon. I parked my car and helped Mckai and Annyn out so that we didn't spill the boxes everywhere.

I looked at the parking spot next to me. It was reserved for the handicapped. However, there was no handicap placard nor any handicap sticker on the car occupying it. People like that make me sick. I put the lanyard with my keys on it around my neck. I looked at its green and blue stripes. My Aunt Nannette bought it for me, along with my car. Aunt Nannette was like a mom to me. She treated me like her own daughter more than my parents ever did. I loved spending time over at her house and playing with my cousins Wren, Coita, and Shirina.

Before we went inside, Mckai asked, "Are you sure that lady isn't scamming us?"

I answered, "Even if she was trying to scam us, there isn't that much to take. The earthly possessions we have don't mean anything. I just want to keep you two and myself safe, and right now this lady is the only chance we have. I am willing to take this chance, as risky as it may seem. She's all we have right now. It's a glimmer of hope."

Mckai and Annyn nodded their heads in agreement. I told them to walk in front of me, and then we headed into the restaurant.

I walked in and I could see the lady in the back of the kitchen. She looked at Mckai, Annyn, and me, and whispered something into one of the cooks' ears. She walked around the counter and approached us. She greeted us by saying, "Hello girls, my name is Sutton Hobson. You can take a seat in that back booth. My break is in a half-hour, and then we can have a talk. Does that sound okay?"

I nodded my head and replied, "That sounds wonderful. My name is Kiely Cosmosis, and these are my sisters, Mckai and Annyn Cosmosis."

"Well, it is very nice to meet you girls." Just as that came out of Sutton's mouth, she looked at Mckai and Annyn eating their food. Then, she turned her attention back to me and asked, "Kiely, did you get anything to eat?" I shook my head no, and she said, "Well, order some food, and I'll have them take it out of my check."

I was amazed at this woman's offer. I felt like such a heel, such a burden. However, she was offering, and I didn't want to pass it up. I think Sutton knew what I was thinking. She told me, "Kiely, it's okay. I am not hurting in any way financially. Tell me what you want, and I'll bring it to you."

"Thank you, Sutton. May I please have a small Coke, a small fries, and a cheeseburger with ketchup?" I responded.

Sutton showed her toothy smile and declared, "One meal for Miss Kiely coming right up!" She waddled away behind the counter, and Mckai, Annyn, and I took a seat in the booth she had pointed us to. We sat down, and Mckai and Annyn gobbled the remainder of their food quickly. They got up to throw their trash away, and while they were in the bathroom, I put my face in the palm of my hands and started crying. I couldn't believe how my life was unfolding right now.

On the surface I may seem pathetic, but trust me when I say I know people have gone through worse. I don't need that cliché speech. However, people are like plates of food when it comes to hardships. You could be a strong glass plate that holds all of the food and balances it well. You could be a paper plate that is flimsy and doesn't have the easiest time holding it all together. Or you could be a Styrofoam plate that completely melts when something hot is put on you. I am the Styrofoam plate. I don't do well with pressure, not in the least. I decided I'd run to the car really quickly and grab my diary before Sutton came back with my food and Mckai and Annyn came back from the bathroom.

I walked briskly to the car and unlocked it. I opened my car door and grabbed my diary. I went back inside the restaurant and saw Mckai and Annyn standing in front of the indoor playground structure. There were two other kids in there, and Mckai and Annyn are two of the shiest kids I have ever met. They just needed a little push. I sashayed over to them and said, "Nobody's going to bite you. Those two kids are probably nervous and afraid to talk to you too. Go have some fun. It's okay." They gave me a hug and ran up the neon yellow steps.

I stared at the ominous clouds that were in view from the windows. The clouds were a dark gray, and the sky was darkening too. There was a massive storm about to erupt, and I was happy to know that I wouldn't have to be in my car to witness it. I made my way back to the chemical-smelling table—a sign it had been washed—and Sutton was already on her way with a tray. Everything I ordered was on it, and it was making my mouth water to the high heavens. Sutton gave me my tray and drink. My Coke was freshly poured and bubbling like Sutton's personality.

She complimented, "What gorgeous eyes you have! I always tell people that the eyes are the windows to the soul. You must be as beautiful on the inside as you are on the outside."

I cringed inside after she said that. Was she trying to hit on me? I was still a minor, technically, and she looked like she was in her thirties! Or maybe I was being über-paranoid because she was a stranger and I watch *Forensic Files* religiously. Whatever the case may be, I had to be careful and decisive. I needed to make a decision soon on whether I was going to put any more trust toward her.

Sutton sat down across from me in the booth and stated, "My boss let me start my break early. So, spill everything that you need to. There is zero judgment here. Tell me what's so bad that you don't think anyone could help you."

I took a deep breath and explained everything that had happened today up until this point. I ended my story by saying, "See, we are out of luck. I wanted to rent a motel room, but I had just enough money to pay for Mckai and Annyn's lunch today." I kept looking at Sutton, expecting her to direct me to a homeless shelter or to suggest calling my parents and making amends. Despite the fact that those options would be the easy way out, I would have to swallow my pride and accept that my parents' views about me were correct.

Yet again it seemed like Sutton could read my mind. "Kiely, I know we just met, and there is no reason you should trust me. I know that to you I am just a stranger who bought you lunch and flashed some smiles. It doesn't constitute grounds for trust, I realize this. However, I want to propose an opportunity to you. An opportunity that would benefit you and your sisters, and it would show your parents that you can take care of yourself. Show them how strong a woman you really are. Come live with me, you and your sisters. I am pretty well-off money-wise. My dad left me with a fortune when he passed. I work here because I get bored. I have no family, or friends for that matter, to share my wealth with and kindness to. Come live with me. I can support you and your sisters. Look, I know this sounds sudden and risky. Please think about what I am offering. It could be a ticket out for you three."

I responded, "Sutton, that's huge. That could be just the thing we need right now. I don't see us getting anywhere without help, and even as parlous as this situation seems, I am going to decide to put my trust toward you. I don't see what other options I have. If I leave with Mckai and Annyn, eventually I will run out of gas. I have nowhere to go and no money to pay for anything. I am so grateful for your generosity. I don't know what to say."

"Just say yes. It could be good for all of us to have someone right now. Mckai and Annyn have you, and you and I have each other. I will protect you. I promise."

"Okay, yes."

"Great. Then it's settled."

Sutton got up from the table and came over to me, and gave me a big squeeze. Maybe Sutton wasn't the predator I thought she was. I was overreacting as usual.

"Well, Miss Kiely, my shift ends at four, so it'll be a couple more hours before we go anywhere. If you need anything, come up to the register and ask for me. I'll be back in no time, and then we'll go home."

I smiled from ear to ear. Sutton went back to work, and Mckai and Annyn were playing their hearts out on the play structure. I decided to write in my journal while I waited.

I opened my journal and read some of my old entries instead.

So I just got this notebook from my new counselor, and I am seriously dreading every wretched week I have to be there. Counselors are such a joke! I mean, c'mon, they are obligated to act nice and all smiley if they want to be paid. They have to act the part in order to actually have a patient. Maybe my counselor is the real deal, but I'm not sure yet. She's actually trying, mentioning we could move the conversations outside if it made me more comfortable. I guess I'll have to see.

I am so pissed at my parents. They drill negative thoughts into my head 24/7, and yet when I feel the same way—when I try to harm myself—they act so surprised that something like that happened. They suddenly care now because if I did harm myself and pass away, their little socialite friends would look down on them. Their egos are way bigger than their love for me, hands down. Why can't these counselors see that I am never going to get better when I was never worse? I want to die. I have or am supposed to have freedom in this damn country.

All the time people are asking doctors to pull their plug, to stop trying. Why can't they do that one simple thing for me? My parents and sisters have told me what seems like a thousand extra times more than usual that they loved me ever since I got out of the mental clinic. Now, I have always known my family loved me. Well, maybe just my sisters. I knew that fully and completely when I attempted suicide, and I know it now. The thing is, I don't deserve to be loved. I'm a lazy-ass, rotten-tempered, piece of class A shit—all things that my parents have called me.

My family is always talking about being strong, overcoming the odds and things that life throws at you as a family. So what puzzles me is why can't they let me kill myself. They're strong. They'd quickly get over me. They don't need me. I'm just the mistake my parents made the first time they had sex, so they probably thought, "We should try again for a better baby," and Mckai came along. Then, I must've unleashed so much disappointment that they needed to have Annyn as well to make up for how much of a letdown I was.

I don't understand why counselors and everyone are so trigger-happy for coping skills. Like, they must say to themselves at night, "Ooh, we've got a messed-up kid. Bet we can fix them up with some good, old-fashioned coping skills." Hell to the no. My dad mentioned how messed up the driveway of the counseling center was, and as soon as he said that, I thought to myself, almost as messed up as I am. My caseworker, whatever her name is—I think it's Alicia—seems like that girl in high school who was a superficial, fake bitch who was fake nice to everyone just to gain popular status. She seems like the kind of person who would talk behind my back or do secret pranks to make my life a living hell just because of the plain thought that she was better than everyone else. Well, look where she is now. Fucking trapped in this tiny town, dealing with people who are depressed because she still hasn't stopped being the bitch she was from high school.

Like, let us die! That's all we want. Like, we've just met this counselor who's trying to tell us that we're important, that we matter, that everyone matters. Well, first of all, I have never seen this chick before today and probably won't after my counseling is done. I won't have impacted her life in any way, so why would she care if I committed or not? I knew why, actually. Because they need to be paid. They don't want their company to have a bad reputation. Sucks that most people are getting sucked into this "everything will get better" bullshit. The fact is that life sucks and will forever suck. My stomach hurts from worrying all the time anyway, and now popping anti-depressant pills is making me sicker than usual. That's a load of crap if I have ever seen one. I shouldn't have to feel any more pain. When is my emotional and physical pain going to end? There has to be a release!

I finished Glee! I know, my life's goal is accomplished. But seriously, if I ever do decide that I had reasons to live, I would want to be an actress or something like that. But as it is, I am me. No one is ever going to know my name unless it's in the obituary section of a newspaper. Then, they'll forget me within a matter of seconds. I'm never going to make it big. I had a few lead roles in my school plays under my belt, but that doesn't mean shit. Just some stupid roles in a lowly high school play played by me, a below-average person.

Mom and Dad made some sausage patties, fries, and popcorn chicken for dinner. It was some killer food, so delicious. I've been trying to watch what I eat because I am as fat as a forty-year-old man with a beer belly.

I hated it at the mental clinic. They constantly checked our weights. They claimed they were not a medical hospital, but then why all the weighing? That's what I call fat-shaming. Honestly, why else? All the workers there are anorexics who need to fat-shame some mental patients for an ego boost. Also, it doesn't hurt that all the shaming benefits the business of the mental clinic.

I hopped in the shower and got scrubbed quickly. I ran upstairs to my room and lay down on the bed. I had the air blasting, and I was in a pair of shorts and an oversized T-shirt. Comfy as hell. Writing is such an escape for me. It helps me speak/communicate things to people that I most probably would never say out loud. I'm thinking about writing actual short stories in this notebook, but I don't know just yet. I've been listening to "Bad Guy" by Billie Eilish for over an hour on an endless loop. I love her music so much. Mainly, I love listening to music by myself because I can play a song as many times as I want, and nobody can say shit about it.

I am so done with some people. They want to talk shit about others even though they're shitty themselves. Like, what the hell? Hypocrisy at its finest. My foot is getting numb because my fat ass is sitting on it. I literally look like a hobo off the streets. Speaking of the poor, it makes me completely sick to my stomach that some people are starving on the streets whilst others buy $8 million homes and have more money than they could use in seven lifetimes. My labyrinth of hair looks like a rat's nest.

More on the topic of music, I mainly listen to music based on my mood. If I am sad, it's sad music; happy mood, happy music; and so on. In other times, when I used to care about my depression getting better, I did that so I could get confirmation that I was not alone in my situation. Now, at this point, whatever makes me want to play it sixteen times over, I listen to it.

So, I just looked at myself in the mirror. I totally look like a hippopotamus in this grey shirt. Ugh. I wish I was pretty. People can tell me that I am pretty or beautiful all they want, but it won't change my looks, and it sure as hell will not change my opinion.

I'm just plain ugly. I always look like trash—no, no, the WHOLE DUMPSTER! Whatever, I mean it's not like my bedroom walls judge me. Well, now that I think about it, they probably do judge me. Even though they are lifeless, inanimate objects, they would still find a way to judge me. Always. Well, I am tired of being awake for another day, so yeah. So for today, I'm calling it good night.

Sincerely, my wretched self @ 10:53 p.m.

P.S. Does grammar matter in suicide notes? Or am I allowed to use run-on sentences and fragments? I'm just being facetious.

I started tearing up. This entry was from last year, after I had gone through losing relatives, verbal abuse from my parents, and so much more. I have had enough, and I was done being all flowers and sunshine. I was at the lowest possible point in my life, and I tried to harm myself over and over. My parents had me checked into a clinic for a while, and I dreaded every single second of it. If anything, the group therapy and the medication—everything about that whole experience—just doubled every bad thought I had. Being able to come home and see my sisters, seeing how deeply hurt and miserable they were when I wasn't there, made me change. I couldn't let my mental health deteriorate that low ever again, especially with all these drastic changes happening in my life right now.

This notebook was given to me by the counselor I was recommended to see after I was checked out of the clinic. After my stubbornness subsided a little bit, I let my guard down, and she helped me so much. I saw her four more times after that first entry, and then my parents told me she was murdered by her husband. They tried to find another counselor for me, but nobody else could help me the way she did so eventually I stopped going to any counselors at all. It has been a lot of work to restore my mental health, but I am trying. Day by day I am better. It's not easy. Oh boy, it is not easy.

I look up from my notebook and over to the registers where a tall, muscular man ordered his food. He was very sarcastic to the workers, and he showed them complete and utter disrespect. I hoped that they would spit in his hamburger. Who hurt him so badly that he felt the need to degrade McDonald's workers to make himself feel better? Whenever I get to meet new people or see strangers, I always wonder if they were the same way as kids. I know people change; I've had quite a lot of experience with it. But what all shaped them into the person they are today? I have always thought it pretty neat that if you changed even the most insignificant moments in your life, you'd be a completely different person from what you are now. If you zigged instead of zagged, where would you be? Mind-blowing. Incredible, actually.

Though, of course, it's the most insignificant things that lead to the important moments, so it's all in how you act leading up to those things. I flipped to another page and read on because what else was I supposed to do to fill the gap of time between now and when we went with Sutton?

Thursday, May 9

So, today was class A shit for the most part. This morning I shaved and fixed my hair real nice. I picked out a dress and slid it on. I wanted to feel good about myself for once. I wasn't doing this for anybody but myself. When I got on the bus, my bus driver made the bus jerk forward before I was even able to sit down, causing me to fall into my seat, which was hella embarrassing. Half of the bus got to see my tighty-whities. First period went fast; we were being lectured on our end-of-year work standards for class.

My next class was choir, and out of nowhere this girl in my class, Shawntae Cranston, started crying. She left the room, and of course my choir director had to follow her out. A teacher from the language arts hallway came in and watched our class as we continued practicing our songs for the concert. There was a huge catfight in the hallway after fourth period let out, so teachers were breaking things up, yelling at everyone to get to class. I went to math shortly after that ordeal, and we had a vocabulary test which sucked because our own math teachers admit that they only use the math terminology/theorems/systems/ideas in the classroom and not in their outside life.

So why the hell are we expected to give a care about long, wordy theorems that mostly don't apply to anything in the real world? Why can't they teach us to balance a check or change a tire? Whoever these so-called "geniuses" were who made all of this malarkey up are some seriously nerdy, high-class know-it-alls who made a random idea sound smart so they can have their name in the history books. After math class, I went to gym class where we had to run a mile. This morning, one of the only pants I can run in without them falling down to my knees was in the dryer. I put them in the dryer last night knowing they'd be fresh and warm in the morning. I tried to take them out this morning, but they were damp. Somebody had shut the dryer off at some point after I went to bed.

So I had to grab my other pair, which had a small chance of totally falling off my body and embarrassing myself yet again. I got changed in a stall in the locker room of the gym, and we all walked over to the track. On Tuesday, I walked the entire track with Joycilynn Bardeau, Ona'liyah-Nichole McLeod, Krelix Mark, and

Laykhenn Upchurch. I was planning on running with them as well. It helped me to run with a group because then I had motivation to do better and catch up and I could talk through the running pains. I didn't want to run by myself and be a bigger loser than I already was. We get out to the track, and the gym teacher tells us that this is a practice day to teach ourselves about pace and endurance. So that means we'll probably have another track day in the future for a grade. He gave us some pace strategies, and the one I used was to run the curves and walk the straights.

So, I did that with Joycilynn, Ona'liyah-Nichole, Krelix, and Laykhenn. We finished dead last at thirteen minutes and thirty-five seconds. Lunch rolled around, and I changed back into my dress. Laykhenn (he's one of my oldest and dearest friends) was back to his old self. He had dated this toxic girl for a while, and she had him under his thumb. He hadn't talked to me for a while, but he broke up with her a few days ago, and it's quite amazing how much happier he is now. We were back to joking and laughing again, as if nothing ever happened. That girl was out of sight, out of mind.

Laykhenn was dating that toxic girl while I was in the clinic, so he had no idea that I had been there at all. He thought I was out sick. I decided to tell him today about everything. We decided to make a suicide pact. We spit on our hands and shook. I was serious, and so was he.

He asked me, "Kiely, what is the worst-case scenario if I jumped from a thirteen-foot building?"

I said, "At the most, you'd be paralyzed or maybe die if you landed on your head or somewhere fatal. At the least, you would break some bones, maybe a fracture or two. Or maybe you wouldn't get hurt at all."

Looking disappointed, he then asked, "What would happen if I were to run my golf car directly into a tree?"

I told him that without a seat belt, he would pose the risk of flying out of the golf cart and smashing his head in. At the least, with a seatbelt, maybe he'd get a broken bone. However, with a seat belt he shouldn't be harmed at all. Then, we proceeded to talk about injecting motor oil into our arms because he said that it would make our livers fail and extreme health problems would soon arise. Laykhenn took my pen and shoved it deep into his leg until the point of making it bleed. He gave me the pen, and I did the same.

Laykhenn and I would fist bump each time one of us would come up with a new, unique way to kill ourselves. The more pain we felt, the better. Joycilynn, Ona'liyah-Nichole, and Krelix said they would never forgive us if either one of us died. As we were talking, one of the biggest bitches at my school, Eriella Grilli, approached me at my table. She whispered in my ear, "You look very pretty today, but black underwear probably wasn't the best choice." She ran back to her table, snickering with her friends. Luckily, Laykhenn didn't hear a thing. My face got hot after such embarrassment. My dress was light pink, and I made sure to put on a white bra and underwear. I checked myself in the mirror this morning ten times before I left the house. Eriella must've been having a piss-pot day, and decided I was an easy target to project her anger onto.

Lunch ended soon after, and I went to the second half of my math class. My math teacher, Mrs. Harris, assigned us a surprise quiz. In the middle of the quiz, Mrs. Phillips, the choir director, came in and asked to take me out into the hallway. I came out the door, and Mrs. Phillips said, "You're not in trouble, sweetie. I saw that your dress was inside out, and I didn't want you to be embarrassed by other students."

I started feeling the biggest wave of dread. I must have put it on wrong after gym because I was in a rush. Mrs. Phillips could tell my mood had dropped, and she said, "It's not that noticeable, but the pockets just give it away. Nobody else probably noticed." I thanked her, and went to the bathroom to fix my dress.

I picked a stall and locked the door. I started crying, I felt like I could throw up. I am such a dumbass. What kind of person doesn't notice that their dress is inside out? I came out of the bathroom, and it seemed like Mrs. Harris was waiting for me. She pulled me into an empty classroom and asked me if I was okay. I didn't feel like spilling any tea to her, so I lied and said I was fine. Then, we went back to the classroom so

I could finish my test. Over the loudspeaker, Principal Ortiz reminded all the teachers that all choir students were released for the rest of the day to practice a whole run-through of the songs for the choir concert tonight.

I gathered my books and left the classroom. I shoved my books into my locker, and a crowd of people were already in front of the choir door. I looked through the swarm of people for Joycilynn, Ona'liyah-Nichole, Krelix, and Laykhenn. Finally, I found them. After all of our choir students were rounded up, we all headed to the auditorium with Mrs. Phillips. Krelix and Laykhenn both needed to finish their literature circle books for class, and they planned to read them while the soloists practiced.

I suggested, "Why don't we try to cut ourselves with the paper of the book?"

Laykhenn was in love with that idea, but it didn't work that well. Laykhenn talked to Joycilynn for a while, asking her questions about the reading. He couldn't ask me because I was in an honors class. Krelix decided to read his book to me, just for fun to pass the time. Soon, we all had to stand up on the stage and sing our rehearsed songs. After the rehearsal was done, we were dismissed to the buses. I gave each of my friends a hug, and I told them that I loved them.

Laykhenn pulled me inside and told me that he would call me tonight before the concert. He told me he was ready to do the suicide pact with me. I thought he was joking so I played along and told him that I would wait for his call.

I sat and looked around at McDonald's. It felt like everyone's eyes were on me. I started sobbing so hard that I started shaking. I had never finished this journal entry, and it was for a very tragic, grisly reason. Last year, on that day, I didn't listen for a phone call. I took a shower and got ready for the choir concert. I expected to see Laykhenn there and to laugh with him the whole night. I arrived at the school, and I found Joycilynn, Ona'liyah-Nichole, and Krelix. I asked them if Laykhenn showed up, and when they had said he hadn't, I shrugged it off. His dad was an alcoholic, and he had to wait for his dad to pass out before he could take the car out. His dad hated the idea of Laykhenn driving in his precious car. I would've taken him to the concert myself, but my parents drove me, and they looked down on Laykhenn.

I had a blast at the concert. We had worked so hard for so many months, and we were finally able to perform for the community. It felt amazing to showcase our talents. That feeling of applause and excitement from the crowd is unique on its own. I waited for Laykhenn to show up. I figured he'd get here shortly after the solos were underway. However, Laykhenn never showed up to the choir concert. I arrived home late at night and skipped up to my room. I checked my phone, and it said there was a missed call from Laykhenn from before the concert started. I listened to the message, and right off the bat I knew something was wrong. His voice was shaky and scared. You could tell he was crying.

Hey Kiely, it's me. I love you so much, Ki. You know that; at least I hope you do. I can't stand it any longer. The pain is too much for me, Ki. I am so sorry. You are my best friend, and I would never want to do anything to hurt you. I just can't stand it anymore. Please understand. Please choose to live. You are so smart and beautiful; you deserve a life full of happiness. Please, please live for me. I love you, Ki. Please forgive me.

Immediately after the message ended, I vomited on the wastebasket near my bed. A wave of dread washed over me. I ran to my parents' bedroom and grabbed the keys to the car out of my mom's purse. My mom and dad were yelling at me, begging for an explanation. I ran out to the car and started it. I left the driveway, and I sped down the road as fast as I could to Laykhenn's house. I finally got to his house and parked as fast as I could. I ran up the doorsteps and knocked hard on the door. His dad answered, and he appeared to be sober for once. His dad is like *Dr. Jekyll and Mr. Hyde.* When he is drunk, he is violent and angry. When he is sober, he is the sweetest man alive.

"Kiely, it's so good to see you. What brings you here so late at night? Are you all right?" asked Laykhenn's father, Dimitri.

I grabbed my phone and cried as I played the message. We both ran as fast as we could to Laykhenn's bedroom. His dad tried to open the door, but it seemed to be locked. Dimitri backed away and rushed to the door, slamming his entire body weight against it. He was able to bust the door down, and I walked into the bedroom first. What I saw was going to haunt me for the rest of my life.

When I walked into the bedroom, I could see Laykhenn on the bed. He was covered up to his elbows with a soft, embroidered quilt. I took a step to the left, and I could see his face more clearly. There were tens of bottles of pills surrounding him, and all of them were empty. I dropped to my knees and did the technicolor yawn, as did Dimitri. Dimitri stepped over me, and as he wailed, he checked for a pulse. There was nothing. Dimitri raced to the phone and dialed 911. As we waited, I screamed and wept. I banged my fist on the headboard of Laykhenn's bed. This was all my fault. I was cracking jokes with him at school today, telling him different ways he could commit this unspeakable act. Never in my entire life did I think he could do it.

Dimitri got on the floor beside me and held me close. I caterwauled for what seemed like hours. After all the screeching and sobbing, my throat hurt as if someone took an icepick and jammed it through my jugular. The paramedics and police came soon after we called, and they came into Laykhenn's room to take him to the hospital. I crawled into a corner and watched them take Laykhenn away. Dimitri followed them downstairs, and I sat there on the floor, shaking with guilt, fear, grief, and sadness all piling on at once. A paramedic found me and helped me stand up. I explained everything, and she held me in a tight embrace until I was ready to let go. She assured me it wasn't my fault. I didn't believe her. I knew the truth.

I went home, and my parents were in the living room waiting up for me. Mckai and Annyn were already in bed.

My mom asked, "Where did you go this late at night? You know that you're not supposed to take our car keys willy-nilly. You are supposed to ask us first!"

I fell to my knees right in front of them. I rested my head on my mom's lap and told my parents every last detail. They were speechless, as I figured they would be. My dad ran his fingers through my hair, and my mom sat in silence. We sat there in place for hours until finally, my mom spoke.

"Kiely, I love you. Please promise me you will never again do anything to harm yourself or to take your life. Please. I cannot imagine what Laykhenn's father must be going through."

I nodded my head and got up from the floor. I told my parents that I loved them, and I headed for the bath. I picked out some comfortable clothing and walked to the bathroom. I filled the bath with steaming water. I found a small bottle of bubble bath, held it over the tub, turned it upside down, and tapped on it so that the liquid soap would stream out of the bottle. I slid out of my clothes and tossed them into the corner. I set my phone down by the sink, and I stepped into the tub.

The warmth of the bath was soothing, as if it was trying to tell me that everything was going to turn out all right. I wasn't sure what was going to happen. If Laykhenn died tonight, I was going to be in a world of hurt and misery. I sank into the bath and stayed underwater for a long while. I stayed under there until my head felt like it was about to explode. It was thrilling knowing my life was in my hands. I could stay under the water a bit longer and let myself run out of oxygen, or I could push myself up out of the water. I decided to get out of the water. I sat up and fixed my hair so that it was out of my face.

I breathed heavily, and I was about to shampoo my hair when I heard my phone ring. I hoped that it was Laykhenn about to tell me some dark humor. I hopped out of the tub and wrapped myself in a towel. I dried my hands and picked my phone up. I was so excited by the sound of the ringing and the thought of hearing Laykhenn's voice, I didn't even bother to check the caller ID. I answered it, and on the other end of the line was Dimitri. The feeling of him answering was so disheartening. I heard him sobbing, and I started tearing up. In a span of five minutes we were both crying loudly, and neither of us had said a word. I knew what Dimitri was going to say, but I didn't want to hear it. I couldn't handle it.

"Kiely . . . My son is gone," Dimitri uttered between sniffles.

I screamed at the top of my lungs. The pain from losing him coursed through my body; it didn't seem real. My eyes were blurred from all of the tears that came spilling out. This couldn't be real. It *wasn't.* Because if it was real, it would mean I would never see him again. It would mean that I pushed him to suicide. We laughed at the thought of suicide, and we cracked jokes about it. Oh god. How could I do that? Oh god. Oh god.

I hung up on Dimitri and lay on the floor, wrapped in my towel. I lay there weeping until I cried myself into slumber. I woke up in the morning and found myself with a massive headache. I picked myself off the floor and slid on the clothes that were meant for bedtime. I pulled a stool that was stored in the corner and put it in front of my bathroom mirror. I sat on the stool and examined myself. I looked like a sleep-deprived raccoon. Instead of acknowledging the harrowing reality that was Laykhenn's death, I focused on the wild dream I had last night.

I had fallen asleep an epitome of teenage existence. I was dressed in a silky, purple evening gown, and I had cried so much my mascara dripped down my face, making it look as if my skin were melting. The ball had made me believe true princes were never real. I skipped into my mom's room, hopeful she'd have something to say to help encourage me. She was passed out again with some rando sniffing her pillowcase in the corner while injecting himself with what smelled like gasoline. I didn't feel like digging another gravesite today. The guy stared up at me and managed a smile before he rolled over and died.

I put my arms under him and dragged him to the back of my house. I dug and dug until my arms felt limp as noodles. I rolled him into the grave and quickly filled it. His soul would forever remain at our house, under the ever-growing willow tree. I looked up at the man in the moon, and he winked at me. He jumped down from the moon and onto my roof. There was such a loud, resonating sound that maybe it could even wake the man under the willow tree. I plead, "Please take me with you."

He opens his mouth wide to smile, and all I could see for miles was his long, razor-like teeth. "Liliosa, don't worry my sweet girl, you have a purpose here. Try to find it," he tells me calmly.

21

A deep, sickening feeling plummeted to my stomach from my throat. I screamed, "PLEASE! Moonie, you have to help me! I'll never belong here. I'm not like them!"

Moonie Man grinned and closed up his jaw, releasing his teeth back into his mouth. The Moonie Man jumped back up to the moon and left me alone.

I woke up, trying to decode what that dream meant exactly. In my dreams, I had a whole different life, and my name was Liliosa. Right now it was just easier to distract myself with that instead of focusing on my reality. I brushed my hair and broke down crying.

I had stayed home for three weeks, and all I did for those three weeks was stay in bed and use the restroom. The only day I didn't was on the day of Laykhenn's funeral. That day, I felt like a shell of a person. I was going through the motions as I applied my makeup and put on my dress. I went to the funeral and looked at Laykhenn's body for about ten minutes. I gave him a kiss on the cheek and put a flower into his coffin. I embraced Dimitri for a long time, and then I moved aside to let others grieve.

I felt a hand pull me into an empty side room, and when I looked, Ona'liyah-Nichole, Krelix, and Joycilynn were staring back at me. I walked forward to give Joycilynn a hug, and she slapped me across the face. All three of them looked like they were fuming with rage.

Ona'liyah-Nichole wailed. "Kiely, what the hell did you do? He asked you specific questions on how to kill himself, and you answered! You basically told him to take those pills! We told you that if either one of you died or both, we wouldn't forgive you. I just can't. You joked about something that serious, and it cost Laykhenn his life! He will never get to marry or to have kids. He loved you, Kiely. He loved you, and instead of trying to help him, you let him continue going into his little rabbit hole. You desensitized suicide and made it seem like it was a cool, funny thing to do. You are a murderer. Don't ever talk to us again."

All three of them walked away, and it felt like I had been punched in the stomach. I stood against the wall and sunk to the floor. They were never going to forgive me for this. *Ever.* I mean, why should they? I sat there for a few minutes before Dimitri walked into the room. He sat on the floor next to me. He held my hands in his and said, "I heard what those kids said. You are far from a murderer, trust me. Countless things went into Laykhenn's death. *Countless.* Hell, I feel responsible for his death. I am drunk more often than not, and that had to have taken a toll on him. Please, please do not blame yourself for his death. You and I heard that message that he left for you. He loved you so much that the last words he ever spoke were for you. If anything, you were the thing keeping him alive. I don't know what straw broke the camel's back, but I know for goddamn sure that it wasn't you."

I replied through tears. "It . . . It just feels like I can't breathe. I am smothered by the thought that I will never be able to talk to him again. I don't know how I am going to get through this."

"Kiely, I know that it seems impossible to live without him. Trust me, honey, I know that more than anybody else. I know I am an unfortunate excuse for a father most of the time, but I did love him. He was my son, and nothing can ever break a bond as special as that. This is going to be hellacious, but we need to let ourselves grieve. We cannot bottle our feelings up. *Ever.* If we do, our feelings will bubble up inside and eventually boil over. We will end up like Laykhenn, and you are too bright and kind of a kid to go so soon. I will be here with you during every step of the grieving process. I failed Laykhenn. I cannot fail you too. We will get through this together, I promise you. We have to let grief in. Grief has a lot to teach us. Please know that you can talk to me about anything. Please live for Laykhenn. He'd want you to be happy. He'd want you to choose to live." I laid my head on Dimitri's lap and cried heavily.

After the funeral, Dimitri made good on his promise. We talked to each other all of the time; he helped give me purpose. Eventually, Dimitri started dating a woman, May, and she made him so happy. She raised a light in him that I had never witnessed since Laykhenn passed. Most of May's family lived thousands of miles away, and Dimitri decided he would go with her. He assured me that I could reach him whenever I needed someone to talk to. I helped him and May pack all of their belongings in a compact moving van. I watched as they blew kisses to me and sped off in the distance. I haven't talked to him since the day he left. I wanted him to find joy again. If I called, I would just be bringing him down. I didn't want to ruin his happiness.

Ever since he left, I had to be my own reason to get up in the morning. I had to get up for myself and nobody else. I needed to be a priority. The entirety of my life reminds me of those water squirter games you can find at carnivals. Sometimes you get all of the water in the hole and you win a humongous prize from the top shelf. Other times you miss the hole entirely. Either my family were staple people in my development and happiness, or they make decisions that make me fall deeper than Alice in her famed rabbit hole. Either things go perfectly or I am left feeling like a shell of a person. My life has always been a chaotic carousel, and as each horse passes, my world gets rocked time and time again. Will it ever stop? As much as I try to make myself a priority, some days it is hard to accept I am worthy of living at all. When that happens, I think back to Laykhenn's message telling me to live for him. And I listen. Maybe this whole ordeal with Sutton will create a new beginning for me.

I closed my notebook and looked over to see Mckai and Annyn playing on a phlegm-colored bouncy bridge. I smiled at the thought that Sutton could make those girls' lives much different from what my life was. They could be happy. Hell, *I* could be happy. Imagine that. I looked at the analog clock on the wall. It was more crooked than a cat's ass in the moonlight. More time had passed than I realized. Half an hour more, and we'd be going home. That was so strange to think. The time flew by, and I called Mckai and Annyn to come down from the play structure. Sutton grabbed her things and ran toward us. She seemed so eager to bring us home. "Ready to see your new home, ladies?" she asked. I nodded.

She led us to her car, and we hopped in as fast as we could. As she drove, there was this relaxing silence that settled over us. We were finally able to breathe. Mckai and Annyn had worn themselves out on the play structure, so they slept soundly in the backseats. After ten minutes or so, Sutton said, "I am so amazed you said yes to my offer. Most people would decline; for obvious reasons of course. However, you were brave. You trust me. I have been alone for quite some time, and it is refreshing to know I will have someone in my life to make me feel better."

I got a peculiar feeling in the pit of my stomach when she said *someone.* There were three of us. I quickly shook the feeling. I reduced the feeling to my utter lack of confidence in my life. I am so used to everything falling apart, and it makes me question every detail.
"Have you ever thought of dating?" I implored. As soon as the words came out of my mouth, I knew I shouldn't have asked. There could be so many factors in her life, and I didn't consider any one of them. I kicked myself on the inside.

Sutton responded, "I have trouble finding people that share my passions and inspirations. When I do, the relationships always end tragically. Nobody I have ever been with stayed with me for long. But when I get a girlfriend, I love to read her journals and diaries. I want to learn everything about that person, especially the sad parts that you wouldn't want to particularly share. It's like the other half of the moon that only the sun gets to see. Have you ever loved anybody?"

Again, I had that odd, looming notion that something was awry. She saw my diary when we were at McDonald's, and she sounded like she was directing everything she said at me. Again, I shook it off. I *had* to shake it off. Sutton was our ticket out, and I was not going to let my suspicious mind ruin that opportunity. I answered, "I loved someone once. His name was Laykhenn. He passed away last year, and it hit me hard. We never dated, but we loved each other."

Sutton told me she was sorry and stayed quiet for the remainder of the ride. She pulled into a long, gravel driveway. I closed my eyes because I wanted to be surprised with what the house looked like.

I heard the sound of a garage door, and she parked. I opened my eyes. The garage was enormous. It was a pearl white color with black polka dots. I jumped out of the car fast, excited to see outside of the house. I ran out the garage door and gazed up at the colossal home that stood before me. I could not believe such a charming, beautiful home existed.

Sutton came over to me and teased. "If you keep your mouth open much longer, the flies will start to make a home."

I playfully punched her in the arm and gave her a hug. "Thank you so much."

She gave me a squeeze back and told me that she could pick up my car in the morning with all of our personal possessions.

We walked back into the garage and gently woke up Mckai and Annyn. Sutton shut the garage door before helping us inside. As she opened the door, a splendorous room was revealed. Mckai and Annyn gasped with great volume. I could see their eyes sparkling in awe and wonder. We came inside, and Sutton told us to make ourselves comfortable. There was a glass chandelier hung in the center of the room, a single light in the middle of it. Her green, carpeted floors were so soft and comforting. There was an array of furniture placed perfectly around the room, and it all looked pristine. Untouched. I started crying because I felt so lucky to be alive. Mckai and Annyn wrapped their arms around my legs and held tight. Sutton beamed a smile toward me.

Sutton asked, "I'm going to make dinner soon. What would you girls prefer?"

Mckai and Annyn spouted off tens of different things, and I giggled. I answered, "I would be fine with anything you made. I am just grateful you let us come with you."

Sutton nodded, reassuring me that she wanted us to be here. We weren't going to be a burden to her. Sutton made a proposition. "How about I make dinner, and you girls explore the house? Pick a room, any room you'd like."

Mckai and Annyn squealed with joy, and I mouthed the words "thank you" to her. I took Mckai and Annyn's hands, and we walked down the hallway to be met by a grand, Georgian staircase.

Mckai and Annyn let go of my hands and dashed up the endless steps. I took my time scaling the steps. It all felt surreal. I traced my fingers on the small indentations of the railing.

I listened to the sound of my shoes against each white stair. I thought, *I could get used to this.* I made it to the top and looked around. I was met with rooms of Brobdingnagian proportions. I stepped into the first room on the left and was surprised to see it was bare. No pictures or personal items to show off any semblance of Sutton's personality. There was a brown dresser that was pushed up against one wall. The top was bare, and I wondered what lay inside. I opened each dresser quietly so that Sutton wouldn't know that I was snooping. I found nothing inside except a roll of duct tape and a fancy pair of lingerie in the middle drawer.

There was a queen-sized bed in the middle of the room with white sheets, white pillows, white everything. I saw a small camera on the wall across the bed. I deduced it to being a security camera. Why else would there be a camera in this bare, spotless room?

I walked out of the room in search of Mckai and Annyn. I found them both a few doors down. They had found what looked to be Sutton's bedroom. There was a twin-sized bed with fluffy, pink, pillows, blue sheets, and cartoon-themed blankets. There were intricate paintings hung delicately all over the walls. There was a stack of journals by her bedside. Mckai and Annyn were looking at the paintings, and I sat on Sutton's bed. I flipped through a couple of the journals, and there was a different handwriting in each. Maybe they were from her exes.

Soon, Sutton was calling us three down to dinner. The girls ran downstairs with such haste, you would think they had been starved. I took my time going downstairs. I took one last glance at her room and shuddered when I looked at the empty, bland room. I walked slowly downstairs and into the front room where we had first entered. Sutton had set a table with a floral print tablecloth and fancy china. Sutton motioned me over to the table, and I saw that Mckai and Annyn were already starting to eat.

Sutton handed me a glass plate and told me to eat as much as I wanted to. I sat down in the chair next to Sutton and looked at the array of food before me. There was chicken noodle soup, salad, a pitcher of water, and cake for dessert. I dished a little of everything onto my plate.

Sutton then said, "Girls, I squeezed some fresh orange juice yesterday, and I was hoping you would try it for me."

Mckai, Annyn, and I nodded. Sutton fixed all three of us a full glass, and when she was done, I noticed that there was none left for her to drink. All three of us drank the juice rather fast, and we assured her that it was tasty.

"Sutton, thank you for everything. It all tastes so good and your generosity is incredible and such a gift," I said.

Sutton replied, "Well, I am so glad you are enjoying it because it will be your last one."

Before I could manage any words, I became very tired and I fell into a black abyss . . .

Down.

Down.

Down.

I woke up and looked around me. I was in the bland room that I explored when we first arrived here. It only took seconds for me to remember what happened at the dinner table, and I started to sit up when I noticed something bone-chilling. My arms and legs were secured to the bed with handcuffs. I thrashed around and tried to break the chains. No such luck. I started screaming although I knew that it would be no use. This house was so gargantuan, nobody would ever hear me. Minutes later, I heard a knock on the wall right outside the room. Seconds later, I saw Sutton sashay in front of the bed.

I screamed, "Why am I tied up? Where is Mckai and Annyn?"

Sutton laughed maniacally and wiped a laughter-induced tear away from her eye. She explained, "Well, Miss Kiely, I was thinking I could have a little fun tonight. Well, it'll be fun for me, not so much for you. As for your sisters . . . let's just say they were already taken care of."

I flailed around in utter fear and rage. I screeched, "What did you do to them? You sicko. I swear if you touched a single hair on their heads, I would end your life. Do not test me. I would go to war for them. You should be afraid of me, not the other way around."

Sutton smirked and looked like she was truly enjoying all of this. She made me sick.

"Miss Kiely, you are hilarious. Did you know that? *Hilarious.* You truly think that you'll be able to escape me? *Ha.* Your sisters sure didn't. Oh, what? Does that make you nervous? Does that make you wanna squirm? I bet your insides are being eaten up by all your worrying. That's good. It means you care. Funny thing is, I don't have that vice. Want to see something that will really make you scared?"

Sutton walked out of the room, and I didn't know how long she would be gone. My stomach ached with panic, and I felt truly helpless. I was finally starting to piece things together. The duct tape, the old journals, the bare room . . . It all seemed to add up to a conclusion that made me sick.

Sutton came back into the room, her hands behind her. I was already shaking from anxiety, and I could not imagine what she had in store for me. She pulled a gun fast from behind her and pointed it straight at me. Everything happened so fast and before I knew it my pants were soaked with urine. I started crying with severe anguish and grief. "You killed them, didn't you? Mckai and Annyn! How could you do that? Why?"

Sutton put the gun down on the dresser and said, "Quite easily, actually. They didn't realize what was happening, and before they knew it, there was nothing to know. Two shots and they were gone. Would you like the gory details?"

I cursed and whipped my arms and legs around as hard and as fast as I could manage. No use.

"You're a monster! Do you get your kicks out of filming yourself hurting innocent people? Keeping their journals as some sort of sick trophy? You are going to jail forever!"

Sutton grabbed the gun and walked slowly over to me. She sat on the bed right next to me. "You have a good eye, and your answer is yes. I love watching life drain away. As for going away to jail, that is never going to happen. Do you think you are special? Because boy, do I have a rude reality check for you. You are going to end up the same way all of those other girls did. The same way your sisters did, but they were easier to kill."

As she said that last sentence, I headbutted her, and she stood up fast. She swore under her breath and rubbed her head.

She stepped toward me and declared, "I am not going to waste any more time on you."

I closed my eyes and dug my fingernails into my palm. I whispered childhood prayers to myself and hoped that I would be saved from this mess. Suddenly, I heard a shot ring out, and I felt myself start to fade away. I started to see the light as bright as ever.

CHAPTER 3

CHESNEY OASISCHEI

My phone blinked on, and I grabbed it to see what the urgent news was. I read the headline: "Local Serial Killer Found in Orange County." I was intrigued, so I clicked on the article and perused the entirety of it. Hours ago, while a jogger was taking his usual route, he heard gunshots and alerted the authorities. When the police investigated, they found three young girls who had passed away. The owner of the home was the murderer of the three young girls. It wasn't her first offense either. The law enforcement officers found years' worth of evidence all around the home. I shuddered at the thought. How could someone take someone else's life? It has always puzzled me, and I hope I never understand it.

Hearing that the three victims were girls made me instantly think of myself and my two sisters, Preity and Larken. We had been watching our favorite show, *Bojack Horseman,* when I read the tragic news. I looked down at my sisters who were sitting on the floor. Larken caught me staring and said, "Take a picture, it'll last longer."

I laughed and responded, "Guys, I just want you to know that I love you forever and always. I will always be here for you two no matter what happens."

Preity rolled her eyes and commented, "Are you high?"

We all giggled as I shook my head. Our mom, Geani, casually walked into the room. She smiled at the sight of us girls. She announced, "Girlies, I love your laughter; it is my favorite sound. But . . . I have some terrible news."

We stopped laughing, and I began to develop a horrible feeling in the pit of my stomach. Before my mom could talk, I whispered softly into her ear. "Mom, I love you with all my heart. Don't try to sugarcoat the news for us though. We can handle whatever you have to throw our way." My mom nodded her head with assurance.

"Well, your father and I committed larceny. I know this sounds strange and unreal, but it is very real and very true. All these things we have are all because your father and I are thieves."

I gaped at the thought of her confession. It rocked me to my core. My parents? Thieves? It all sounded too much. My parents were normal. My *family* was normal. How could this be happening? Why was she mentioning this now?

"The truth is all these years of stealing have caught up to us. The police are onto us, and we cannot be here when they locate this house. We all have to be gone far away."

Preity and Larken started to sob, and I rushed to the bathroom. I held my hair back as I vomited in the toilet. I grabbed a tissue and wiped my face as I flushed. After washing my hands, I held my face under the spigot. I felt the cold water soothe me and calm me down. This had to be a delusion. I would go back into the room and find my mom casually watching television with my sisters. Oh, who am I kidding? Only me, myself, and I. I needed to face reality. This crazy situation my mom was saying was true. I had to prepare myself to go back in there and face the facts.

I came back into the room, and my mom was trying to soothe Preity and Larken. Preity wailed, "Mom, don't let them take you and dad away."

My mom rubbed their backs and whispered reassuring things to them. Mom looked up at me and instructed, "Chesney, you have to be the adult now, sweetie. I know it's surprising, frustrating, and sudden, but you need to take care of Preity and Larken. A friend of your dad and mine is coming any minute now to pick him and me up. You'll be staying with Aunt Katrielle and Aunt Mila for a while, just until we can create new identities and throw the authorities off our scent. Go pack your stuff immediately. This will all work out in the end, I promise."

I wanted to say something, but I failed to find any words. I failed to see how any of this nonsense was going to be okay. Preity, Larken, and I slumped off to our rooms; we did not have much, so it was going to be easy to pack. We each had a suitcase from the time we went on a trip to visit with our Uncle Matthias in New Zealand. Oh god. Did our whole family know about our parents' larceny? Everyone but us? I dreaded pulling out my suitcase. It left a deep knot in my stomach. A deep knot that hungered for fear, and once it was fed, it just begged for more. I have not had such a deep knot since the death of my dog, Dunk. I wrote about that day in my journal when it all happened so that I would never forget it. Here's that entry:

Brr . . . The snow was frigid, and the dress I wore didn't help even though I wore a sweater over my shoulders. My head was freezing, and my hair was a labyrinth of knots. My strands were frosted at the tips with snowflakes. I was pacing in my garage, waiting to go to my third grade winter recital. My Grandma Cacamwri wasn't in a rush to leave because she had flown two states over just to see my performance. She wanted to talk to my parents before we left for the recital. Eventually I came back inside and sat inside by the blazing fire.

My ears felt very waterlogged because all I could hear were blurbs of sounds. My gaze was caught in the red-hot fire kindling. There was a comfortable, warm, cozy dog house in my backyard for my dog, Dunk, and he laid in his box. I remember my dad watching Dunk curiously from inside, and his face expressed that he was concerned. My dad fidgeted for a while and finally went outside. It had been snowing for a while, and my dad had to grab his boots and coat.

I constantly badgered my family, asking if something was wrong with Dunk. Suddenly, it felt like the world stopped when I saw my dad crying and pounding his fists on Dunk's house. My dad came inside after wiping away his tears and delivered the horrid news that Dunk died of old age. I blubbered up a storm and almost couldn't stop. I stared out at the moon. It looked like it was grimacing at me, as did all the stars. I figured that Dunk would be up there soon enough. But the show must go on. I attended the concert, and I did it with flair. My kapellmeister, Mrs. Tura, directed us with adroitness. Everything was forgotten for a little while until I got home and the gloominess hit me once again. Dunk was the earth to my ominous moon.

My dad told me that grieving was healthy, but I should realize that Dunk lived a long, eventful life, and he was loved. I didn't know if I could accept that I would never see my dog again, at least not for a long time. Sometimes I wish my heart wouldn't get involved with everything so it wouldn't have to be broken. It's job is to pump blood. That's it. Well, that's not all it's for, but you get the point. Future Chesney, please never forget Dunk. And please, although we may hate it, use your heart as much as possible. Also, Dad has the urn of ashes for Dunk. Make sure he keeps it.

Sincerely, Chesney

I looked around my room and realized that it would probably be the last time I was going to be in this house. That thought didn't hit me as hard as I thought it would. I guess it's because I have to come to realize that family comes before everything. It *has* to be like that. Nothing else compares to family, and without them, I have nothing and would be nothing. They are all I need. Well, I need my friends too, but they are my little group of chosen family. I quickly shoved things into my suitcase and finally zipped it up. I kissed the wall before I left my room, as if saying thanks for the memories.

I went into the hallway and waited on Preity and Larken. Aunt Katrielle and Aunt Mila would be here soon. Everything was happening so fast, and I finally had a second to breathe. Preity dragged her blush-colored suitcase out of her room, and Larken swiftly skipped with her orange suitcase. Mine had a floral print, with my name written on the top with brown marker. I like my name. Most people don't like their name, and I am fortunate to be at peace with mine. Chesney means peaceful, and most of the time, I try to be. My favorite quote is "There is nothing more powerful than a group of determined sisters marching," by Kamala Harris.

My sisters and I need to march into my aunts' house, determined and strong. Preity and Larken walked with me to meet our mom in the other room. She said, "Your aunties are here. My ride will be here soon. They picked your father up at work already."

I wondered who *they* were. My sisters and I went outside without saying anything. How could we? Saying goodbye was way too hard. I did not know how long we would be apart, but I wanted to keep the hope that I would see my parents again, alive and well. I also didn't want to think about my parents having to run in fear for who knows how long.

As we walked out the door, I watched as my Aunt Mila unlocked her door and got out of the car. We got closer to the car, and Aunt Mila took our suitcases and loaded them into the trunk. We all entered the car and buckled up. Aunt Katrielle was in the driver's seat, and she flashed us a look of sympathy and pity. It made me uncomfortable. We were all silent the whole ride, and all I could think about were my friends. Aunt Katrielle and Aunt Mila lived an hour away. I would not be able to see them in person for a while. We are supposed to be keeping a low profile.

All six of my friends had their own unique talents and characteristics. Candi volunteered at the local recreation center to teach tap dance to elementary students. She has always been kind and accepting of everyone who comes her way. Her brass-colored hair is always tied in a low ponytail, brushing across the nape of her neck. She always smells like freshly-baked chocolate chip cookies. She is very gifted when it comes to the visual arts. When she isn't busy running around teaching dance, I always find her painting.

Kyristie is always playing soccer after school, no matter the weather. She always complains about her weight although she's what society's beauty standards would call skinny. She is never *ever* satisfied with her body, and I worry about her mental health all the time. She tries to fit in thirty soccer goals and ten laps around the field each day. Her brownish-red hair is always left loose and free. She claims that it helps her run faster because she feels like a free spirit, an uncaged bird. However, she is exactly the opposite. She *is* a caged bird. She is the bird, and the cage is all of her insecurities. They are blocking her from living her life to the fullest.

Skilynn is as bubbly as sparkling water, and her perky behavior always seems to rub off on all of our friends and me. She was always having a manicure or pedicure done; she is very serious about her nails. Her hair is cut into a neat bob that leveled with her chin perfectly. Whenever one of our friends is sad, she always makes us feel like a million dollars. She absolutely loves birthdays and always buys tubs of ice cream for all of us to share. She insists that we have a sleepover every time one of us has a birthday. We always sprawl across the floor and stretch until our shirts rose above our belly buttons. We usually watch romcoms and always, by the end of the night, finish off the ice cream. She is the rock and glue of our group.

Haiyli is definitely very special to me. I always call her by her full name, Haiyli Anne Maretich, and she always calls me by my full name. It's a little weird thing we do. Haiyli is closer to me than anyone else in our group. We all love each other in our group, but some of us are closer than others. She always has the stench of cigarette smoke following her. She also always has a pack of grape gum in her pocket, and I think she chews it so much because it helps relieve her nerves. We are always chest-bumping and making up silly handshakes. We carefully braid each other's hair almost every time we see each other, and then, like weirdos, try to whack each other with our braids. Haiyli and I understand each other more than the other girls ever could. Haiyli tells me things that she has never told anybody else. I know the skeletons from her closet, and she knows mine. She is my best friend. I wonder how she will be when I am away.

Emailly is the prankster of the group. She is always buying whoopee cushions, flowers that squirt water, and other small gags. Her hair is all the way down to her belly button, and she always dyes it like a rainbow. She is always wearing short-shorts, the kind that has the pockets hang below the actual shorts. Sometimes the pockets bug me so bad that I am inclined to rip them off. She is a devoted friend and always makes us laugh when we are down, and I have always been thankful for that.

Daniyel is the last but definitely never least. She is the shy introvert of the group. With all of us crazies, I wouldn't blame her for being so quiet. Every second of the day, you can catch her reading a book. We try to get her out of her shell and come to do things with us. Usually it works because she cannot read while we are all talking and making it hard for her to concentrate. Daniyel was forgotten at times, and I feel awful admitting that. One time, all of us went to Steak and Shake and sat at a booth. We were all relaxing and such when the waiter came. We all ordered while Daniyel kept her nose in her book the whole time. Finally, we received the food we had ordered. Afterward we left in Emailly's dad's van. We were probably about ten minutes from the restaurant when Haiyli and I looked to the back row to ask if Daniyel finished her book. Surprisingly, she was not there, and we realized that we left her at Steak and Shake. Emailly drove quickly, and when we picked her up we all apologized about a million times.

Anyway, as anyone can see, my friends are very special to me, and thinking that I may never get to see them again is beyond devastating. I snapped out of my own head and realized a half an hour had passed while I was in my thoughts. My Aunt Katrielle was driving slowly and carefully, but suddenly a semitruck came barreling down the road. I assumed that the driver was either drunk or tired because the driving was crooked and over the line. Aunt Katrielle tried to swerve, but the semitruck hit us. We went off the road, rolling and rolling and rolling. My face collided with the window. Steam rose from the back of the car, the smell much too intense to condense into words. Metal on metal. A burning sensation. I felt myself drifting away, and I could see the light as bright as it'll ever be.

CHAPTER 4

KSENIA BLACKWELL

I was swinging on my porch swing, admiring the oak tree that my great grandmother had planted when she was a child. My boyfriend, Zack, sat beside me and held my hand. We were silent, but the silence was a refreshing, comfortable one. My sisters, Hannalyn and Alenya, were laying on the porch and making shapes out of clouds. All I could think about was how poetic and beautiful this moment was. I was a writer myself and often wrote poetry. Often I write about my tragedy and loneliness. With all that happens in the world, I want people to know that they are not alone in their feelings. I wrote a poem titled "Feelings," and it is rather dark. But hey, if it helps someone, that is all that matters, right?

"Feelings" by Ksenia Blackwell

1 See the drowning of the man,
He'll be gone in a three-minute span.
Who is that screaming near the blood?
Is it the one controlling the flood?
The man shudders at the emotionless pool,
Why was the world so heartless and cruel?
Even if the drowning waters are metaphorical,
These feelings are not a mere phantasmagorical.
He isn't drowning in water
But every day he ventures outside, it's like leading a lamb to the slaughter.
He's drowning in feelings.

2 See the drowning of the man,
He'll be gone in a three-minute span.
For in the world,
When your thoughts become unfurled,
You get attacked
Jam-packed
With hateful words.
You start to drown in feelings.

The same sorrow came to that poor man,
Oh, he'll be gone in a three-minute span.

Zack and I watched as the traffic sped down the road, scurrying like rats. One specific car caught my eye. There were five people in the car, and the driver drove rather slowly. I admired that. They were not in a hurry like the rest. Out of the blue, a semitruck came flying down the road, weaving in and out of the lanes. The car of five tried to swerve away, but it was too late. The semitruck and the family of five collided. At first, I didn't know what was going on. The crash did not register in my mind. However, Zack jumped up and Hannalyn and Alenya screamed, and I got pushed back into reality. I stood up and embraced Zack. Tears started rolling down my face.

"Shh . . . Don't cry, Ksenia. It'll be all right," said Zack soothingly.

I rushed inside and grabbed the phone. I dialed 911, and soon enough the paramedics and law enforcement officers came.

After an hour, I still continued crying.

Alenya suggested, "You and Zack should go take a stroll to clear your head." Alenya studied her nails and didn't look at me. She isn't the best with messy feelings. I watched as Hannalyn stayed silent, and I wondered what was going on in her mind. She is fifteen, two years younger than me, and she barely says a word anymore. She used to be full of light and now, I barely recognize her.

Zack asked, "Well, Ksenia, what do you think?"

I picked at my nails and answered, "I think it sounds like a great idea. I need to get away for a little while. Is there anything special happening in town?"

He thought for a while and then remembered. "I believe the car show is going on. That could be fun."

I nodded my head, and we started walking down the sidewalk. We walked hand in hand although my hands were clammy from nervousness about the crash. It took about ten minutes to walk to the car show. When we got there, I spotted my four friends Allycia, Meah, Lorietta, and Keilee eating ice cream on a bench. As soon as they saw us, they sprang up and greeted us with joy.

Keilee yelled, "Oh my Lord in heaven, what happened to you? Your makeup is all smeared, and you look like a drowned rat. Why do I even bother?" Keilee is obsessed with how we all do our makeup as if smeared makeup was more important than how we were feeling. Popularity is something she had always wanted, and she would do anything to get it. It makes me feel worthless, but I have known her so long that it was hard for me to cut ties with this toxic relationship.

Zack got close to Keilee and said harshly, "Never talk to her like that again. You're just mad because you know she is so much better than you. Jealousy is not pretty on you."

Keilee gasped and walked away. This was not the first time that someone had to put her in her place.

Zack whispered into my ear, "Look, I am not sorry I yelled at her. She deserved it."

I nodded, agreeing with him. I looked down at the ground and told Zack that we better get going so that my parents wouldn't worry about where I was. Allycia, Meah, and Lorietta said in unison, "Love you to bits, Ksenia." I told them I loved them, and Zack and I started to walk back to my house. As we edged closer to the porch, we saw that all that remained from the crash was blood and bits of metal dispersed through the grass.

Hannalyn and Alenya were still on the porch, but this time they were on the swing. They did not see Zack and me at first, but when they did their faces became so distressed and concerned. My mom, Priya, and dad, Trae, opened the front door and came to the porch. My mom started angrily tapping her foot, and she chided, "You know that you're supposed to tell me if you are going somewhere. Why would you just leave with Zack? That is so irresponsible of you! I did not know that I raised such a mindless, arrogant fool."

I choked back tears, trying to come up with some sort of witty riposte. Zack surprised me by whispering in my ear. "I better go." I was speechless. Was he just going to hang me out to dry like this? What a coward.

I watched as Zack left, and I stayed silent. My dad intervened in the conversation by saying, "Listen, there is no reason to hurt each other like this. Ksenia, we love you very much. We were worried about you. Zack could have kidnapped you, or you could have been taken away by some pedophile. Too much pandemonium happens in this world, and the hardest job is being a parent in this society. Anything could happen to you, especially since you are a defenseless, naive little girl. Anyone could easily take advantage of you."

I was taken aback. I actually believed that my dad was capable of a sincere apology. I was wrong.

"Do you want to know something? What you have between your legs doesn't constitute the right to be a dick. You are too narrow-minded to believe I could handle myself. I am much stronger and more capable than you could ever imagine. You do not get to decide what I can and cannot handle. I am leaving."

My mom snickered at the thought, and to prove to them that I was committed to what I said, I started walking. My dad was rendered wordless, and my mom asked my dad, "She's joking, right?"

I kept going down the sidewalk, asking myself what I had just done. I was happy that I stood up for myself, but where was I supposed to go? I was five minutes away from my house, when I heard heavy breathing, and I felt a hand touch my shoulder. It was Hannalyn and Alenya.

Alenya said, "We are coming with you. Standing up to the patriarchy and all that." I looked at Hannalyn, and as per usual, she remained silent.

"Well, I am so glad, but I am not sure where we could go tonight. I had a little fight with Keilee, and I think it made the other girls mad. There is no way I can speak to Zack again after he left me like that."

Alenya scratched her head and thought for a couple of seconds. "Hey, what about the park? We can sleep in the slides. I know it is not the greatest plan, but at least it's a plan."

I agreed, and we walked toward the park. It was getting late, and we had to find some semblance of shelter. As we approached the park, Alenya asked, "Will Mom and Dad ever forgive us? For picking our older sister over our parents?"

I answered her, "They will. However, we cannot let them treat us this way. I don't know about you, but pounding insults into us is not the type of parenting style I want."

We made sure nobody was at the park, and it seemed as though the coast was clear. I was not particularly tired, but Alenya seemed exhausted. She found a small swirly slide and curled up inside. She was out like a light in no time at all. It was just Hannalyn and me left.

I figured this was my chance to connect with her. I inquired, "Hannalyn, I know that we are both getting older, and we have different interests. I just don't want us to grow apart any more. Please talk to me. You haven't talked in what seems like ages. Please say something. I love you so much. Please."

Hannalyn took a deep breath. "Each day, a loud wind goes through one of my ears, and I wish it would go through the other. This body of mine has been burning, and it needs to cool down. Burning with passion, with love. Burning for way too long. When will I get my chance to cool down? To freeze my melting heart a bit? The flame should never have to burn its candle's wax so far that the wick incinerates. No flame of mine should be stressing that far. My love, my world. She's forbidden and unaware of my love for her. A dark, empty room becomes whole with a single glimpse of her smile. My love should not have to run out, when the intended user can never use it. My heart burns for her.

"I am young, so the wick of my heart should be new. I fear that soon all of my love will be lost on someone who'll never have it. Bee is her name. It sounds so simple and sweet, like an ice cream cone on a midsummer's day. I dreamt many nights about building a cottage in the country with just me and her. No one else can shout their opinions. It'd just be us together. But, as I had feared, it cannot be as simple as I would like. We are only fifteen, but besides that, all real fairy tales are about a man and a woman. No fairy tale would celebrate a couple like us. I love Bee. I just wish she knew it. Maybe she does know, and she is scared of her parents' reaction.

Oh my lord. What would they do? I have tried to like guys, to be the girl that Mom and Dad want me to be, but I am not that. So I have to pretend. But this pretending stuff is starting to get pretty old, and I am stuck in a continuous loop. I cannot imagine the disappointment Mom and Dad would feel. Disappointment is the worst kind of mad. I've always wondered who Bee liked. She has never dated anyone, never commented on whether or not she found someone attractive. She kept most of her feelings under lock and key. I have so many things on my mind, and it's eating me alive."

Hannalyn started sobbing, and I took her to a set of steps by the bouncy bridge and sat down with her. She rested her head on my lap as she cried. I ran my fingers through her hair, and I started to cry myself. She had to keep this massive secret to herself, and for so long she was alone.

"Hanna banana, I love you so much. No matter what you do, who you love, you are my sister. Nothing is ever going to change that. You mean so much to me and it pains me that I couldn't be there for you. I am so sorry." We sat there for a long while, and finally we laid down in a slide together. I did not want her to be alone tonight.

The morning light shone down on the playground, and when I woke up, Hannalyn was still asleep. I looked at her face, and even in slumber, she seemed pained. I saw two girls about my age walk toward the slide we had slept in. They appeared to be identical twins. The one had a high, slick ponytail, swinging every which way as she walked. The other had her hair dangling down to her hips. That was the only major physical difference I could find between them, but who knows what unique scars, scratch marks, freckles, acne, and such they have? They continued to walk toward the slide and finally stopped at the edge.

Ponytail said, "Hi, my name is Arya Klint. My sister and I noticed that you slept here. We were wondering if you were poor or something. We're relatively wealthy, so we could help you out."

The other sister punched Arya and apologized. "Don't mind Arya. She can be so oblivious with how rude she is. I'm Raeanin. Do you need somewhere to stay? We have a guest bedroom you could use."

I thought about what they had said, and I decided that it was probably the smartest choice to make with our current circumstances. I responded, "That would be great, thank you so much. We're not poor, it's just that—"

Raeanin cut me off. "No need to explain yourself. We'll happily invite you into our home, regardless of the details."

Hannalyn began to wake up, and I told her the plan. We walked over and told Alenya the plan as well. Alenya exclaimed, "We'll have a warm bed tonight!"

Arya and Raeanin shot a sympathetic look toward us as if we were shelter dogs about to be euthanized. I asked, "How far is your house away from here?"

Arya gracefully replied, "Only about two minutes. What's your name?"

I answered, "Ksenia Blackwell. These are my two beauteous sisters, Hannalyn and Alenya."

Raeanin and Arya nodded their heads in unison, and we started the walk to their house. It was not too long until we arrived. Arya was right, they were clearly well-off. The house had a spiffy, paved driveway that held an Audi and a Prius. Who knows what was in the garage. As we walked to the front door, I saw a crystal chandelier hanging in the middle of the ceiling. Raeanin opened the gold-plated doorknob and brought us into their living room.

The living room had hardwood floors and wainscoting. The walls were a calming light blue, and the entire room smelled of fresh apple cider on a winter morning. Their television was an overly large flat screen with surround sound speakers. There were two leather couches, one black and the other tan. There was a clear coffee table with a porcelain mug on top and a few newspapers in a neat stack.

"So," says Raeanin, "Would you guys like to play a board game?"

We all said yes, and I asked, "I don't want to be nosy, but where are your parents?"

Arya explained, "Our dads had a business meeting a couple of states away, and they won't be back for at least a week."

Raeanin left the room for a couple of minutes and brought back a game of Monopoly. We all sat on the floor and decided that Alenya would be the banker.

Arya boasted, "You guys better watch out, I consider myself a board game virtuoso."

We cackled after she said that, and then the game began. Arya set up the game, while Raeanin got fluffy pillows for us to sit on. Alenya started off, then Hannalyn went; next up was me, then Arya, and then Raeanin. Alenya ended up winning, and Arya said it was dumb luck.

We cleaned up all the game pieces, and I sighed. "So, what are everyone's plans for the day?"

Raeanin explained, "Arya and I have dance class for a few hours and then some other tutors. You guys can stay here, or you can go somewhere if you need to. If you need some clean clothes, you are welcome to our closet and our bathroom."

I thanked her and said, "I am probably just going to stay here, freshen up, and relax. Yesterday was pretty hectic."

Raeanin and Arya got up, and each gave me a big hug. Soon they were getting dressed for dance. They left and it was just Alenya, Hannalyn, and I.

"So . . . Hannalyn, how about we score you a date with Bee?"

As soon as I said that, Alenya asked, "Bee Braxton? Isn't she a girl?"

Hannalyn gulped and said, "Yeah, she's a girl. Do you think any less of me?"

Alenya crawled over and gave Hannalyn a squeeze. She sat there for a second before releasing. "I love you just the same."

I was glad that Alenya accepted her. Hannalyn had enough stress worrying about how she would tell our parents. Hannalyn answered my question by saying, "I want to talk to her alone. I am going to get a shower, and then I am going to head over to her house."

I was so proud of my sister. Zack had to ask me if I wanted to go on a date. I was too chicken to say anything to him first. "Go get 'em tiger," I said as I laughed.

Hannalyn stood up from the floor and walked around, searching for a bathroom and some fresh clothes. Alenya started studying her nails, chipping off small pieces of nail polish.

"Look, Ksenia, it's been fun staying here and proving a point to Mom and Dad, but I want to go home," she stated. She looked at me for a few seconds, curious to see how I would react. I was a little hurt, but I understood.

"Go ahead. I love you. Be safe."

Alenya kissed me on the forehead and walked out the front door. Alone at last. I stood up and walked around the house, looking for something to do.

I found a notepad and a pen and started writing some poetry.

"Such a Sad Song - Ksenia Blackwell
When times are getting rough,
I'll eat a candy rabbit made of fluff.
I'll choke on the fluff and die.
That way, I won't tell another lie.
Many more rabbits to come,
Many more rabbits to come and be done.

This poem, I decided, was about bad decisions and deviation. When we are distressed or in a bad place in our lives, we tend to make bad choices over and over. We would like to believe that we have learned, but once shit hits the fan, we are back at it. Life is not lived without mistakes. If we had no mistakes in our life, we wouldn't have lived. Mistakes help us learn what school could never teach. There are people out there who believe that having a higher education makes you wiser, but I do not believe so. I don't believe that all those who are wise had higher education, if any formal education at all. What are the criteria for being wise? What does it mean to you? Does it mean book smarts? Or does it mean being wise because you have gone through life and learned from all your mistakes? I believe book smarts and sagaciousness can be separated. There are many studies that show many scholars and those with higher IQs lack common sense. Those who are wise and have learned from this lesson-filled life rather than solely relying on book smarts are able to truly understand what it is like to have lived.

"Lover; Monster (synonyms)" - *Ksenia Blackwell*
Her eyes sparkled
As she looked my way.
She made my heart flutter
In a way that nobody else has.
As she wrapped me around her finger,
She made me weaker.
She was heaven in the daytime
And hell in the evening.
My lover, my monster.

This poem could be used for anybody, but I wanted it to represent how men can be abused by women just as women are abused by men. People often disregard the validity of male abuse and rape. Men can be used too. They can be "wind-up Romeos," expected to be okay with the snap of a finger. A man should be able to freely feel and express himself just as anyone else does. It's not okay that we as a society dismiss these feelings. We need to accept that men are just as vulnerable. Gender equality, right? We need to realize that men *are* equal to women and vice versa.

"Grief" - *Ksenia Blackwell*
Grief is a trick
That not even the best magicians can pull off.
She takes and takes
Until you are left bare.
As much as you may want to,
Do not rush her out the door.
Invite her in,
She is also able to heal.

Grief can come in many forms. Grief is a sharp arrow, and the target is our heart. Some days it'll miss the target entirely. Some days it can hit us mildly, but on other days, a perfect bullseye. Although we may want to shut our feelings off and drift away, greeting grief and making friends with it is the best option. Grief can teach us to love harder and to be thankful for the people and things that we do have in our lives. It prepares us for the reality that nothing lasts forever, and that is okay.

"Her" - *Ksenia Blackwell*
She makes me blush,
Oh, what a wonderful rush!
Her energy radiates with mine
She makes my insides feel like melting ice cream.
I wish I could hold her forever,
Maybe that day is near.

Just as I was about to start another poem, Hannalyn came into the living room, wearing an oversized shirt with high-waisted jeans. She had her hair straightened, and she wore a pair of butterfly earrings. She chose a pair of black boots with white socks.

"Ooh, you look so pretty. Bee will be swept off her feet."

Hannalyn looked embarrassed as she thanked me for the compliment. Hannalyn gave me a hug and announced, "I will be back later. I love you." Then, she walked out the front door. I thought about writing more poems, but I decided the best option was to get a shower.

I walked out of the living room and walked down the hallway until I found Arya's room. Her name was written on the door with a magic marker. Her room was cherry-scented and had pink carpeting. On a small wooden desk she had some potpourri. There was a wide doorway within her room that led to a mosaic-tiled bathroom. Before heading into the bathroom, I found a white armoire and searched it for some clothes. I chose a tight, lavender dress with black socks. I walked into the bathroom and stripped off all of my clothing.

I turned on the showerhead, and as I waited for the water to heat up, I searched for a washcloth. When I found one, I hopped in the shower and was delighted to be met with warm, relaxing water. *I could get used to this,* I said to myself. I put my head under the water and let it run down my face and all over my body. I found a bottle of blueberry-scented body gel and some fancy, name-brand shampoo. I quickly finished my shower and got into the clothes I picked out. After getting dressed, I looked at myself in the mirror and admired my choice. I was not the type to love my body, but this dress made me feel good about myself for once.

I grabbed my dirty clothes and found a laundry basket to toss them into. I walked back into the living room and lay down on one of the couches. I fell asleep quickly, and when I awoke, I heard Arya and Raeanin talking in another room. I followed the sound of their voices and found what looked to be their kitchen.

"Hey, sleepyhead. You look cuter in that dress than I do," said Arya.

I scratched my forehead and asked, "What time is it? Did Hannalyn come back yet?"

Raeanin answered, "It's five o'clock in the afternoon. You slept like a log; you must have needed it. I haven't seen her. Did she say where she was going?"

"She was going to ask someone on a date. Maybe she got lucky and they went to a restaurant or something," I presumed.

Raeanin responded, "You're probably right. So, Arya and I were thinking about ordering some pizza. Are you cool with that? We'd like to know what toppings you want."

I smiled and said, "Pizza sounds great. I will eat regardless of what you order. I truly appreciate everything you are doing for me and my sisters."

Raeanin grinned and grabbed the phone to dial a pizza joint. I walked into the living room and waited for the pizza to arrive. Arya and Raeanin were busy grabbing plates, soda, utensils, and napkins, so I answered the door when the pizza guy came.

I took the pizzas and hollered for Arya and Raeanin. We sat in a circle and talked as we ate. After an hour or so, Arya commented, "You know, Ksenia, you are a pretty cool chick. I am so glad we know you."

It was incredible to hear; I had felt like such a burden. They were beyond caring for letting us stay here. After we ate, we cleaned everything up, and we decided to take the party to Raeanin's room upstairs. We spent hours chattering, painting our nails, reading magazines, etc. After a while, Arya fell asleep on the floor. Raeanin giggled and said, "She's in such a deep sleep, Alice in Wonderland would be impressed. I am going to lay down, but you are welcome to stay up as long as you want. Good night." She tossed me a blanket and lay in her bed.

I settled down on the floor and curled up with the blanket Raeanin gave me. I fell asleep and woke up after what seemed like an hour. I saw a dark figure by the window, so I rubbed my eyes, thinking it was just an illusion. I realized that it was Hannalyn, and I felt relieved that she made it here safely. I walked over to her as quietly and as softly as I could manage. I did not want to wake up Raeanin and Arya. I touched her shoulder, and she jumped backward. She must have not known I was awake. I whispered in her ear, "How was Miss Bee Braxton?" She didn't answer me, and I saw that she had been crying.

"I went to her house and told her that I liked her, but you should have seen the look of disgust on her face. She called me a worthless dyke and spat in my face. She broke my heart. I can't do this anymore, Ksenia. I can't. How am I ever supposed to show my face again? Maybe I deserved it. Maybe Bee is right. I am worthless," confessed Hannalyn.

I started bawling for her. "Hannakins, I am so sorry. She is so blind, you are incredible. You are going to go so far in life, and you will find someone that makes you so happy. Someday you will soar."

Hannalyn wiped away tears from her face and said, "Not someday. I am going to fly today."

Before I realized what was happening, Hannalyn opened the window and jumped. In a rush of panic, I jumped after her. When I hit the ground, I heard a snap and saw the light as bright as ever.

CHAPTER 5

CAMBER YPPAH

I was in my warm bed, snuggled up in a quilt that my grandmother had made for me with the smell of peppermint wafting in the air from my lotion, when I heard a loud thud next door. I was not used to hearing any noise from my neighbors because the couple was usually out of town, and their daughters were quiet. They never make any ruckus, so I was sure this was an emergency situation. I did not want to wake my mom, Usha, or my dad, Faron, in case I was truly wrong, so I went to my sisters' room. I knocked softly on their wooden door four times before my youngest sister, Aloki, came to the door groggily.

She grunted, "What is it, Camber?"

I said hastily, "Wake Emersyn up, quickly! I think there is something bad going on next door."

Whenever Aloki hears about something that might turn into a possible adventure, it puts a little skip in her step. She pulled Emersyn out of her bed, and quickly kept her up to date with what was happening. Emersyn was trying to look for her shoes, but I pulled her arm and chided, "There's no time for that!"

We tiptoed to the front door, and I unlocked it as quietly as I could manage. Emersyn and Aloki went out first so I could shut the door. Emersyn asked in a loud whisper, "Camber, do you really believe this is a good idea? I mean, it's so dark out here in the cold grass, and—"

I interjected and answered her with a question. "What if somebody was seriously hurt or in danger? Would you rather complain and go back inside when we can help someone?"

Emersyn's face reddened with embarrassment, and we started traipsing to the next-door neighbor's house. I was a teensy bit afraid because I was not sure what we'd find. But I kept telling myself that there might not be anything at all. Grass stuck between my toes. We edged closer to the Klints' home, and I stopped. I fell to my knees when I saw the ghastly sight.

There were two people lying in the grass with their limbs hyperextended. I was mortified. Finally, I stood up and instructed my sisters. "Emersyn, Aloki, please stay where you are while I go see what happened." They nodded in agreement. I walked over to them and realized that they were not the Klint sisters. My heart raced as I bent down to see if they were breathing. I checked their pulse and realized that they had passed away. I screamed. "Emersyn! Aloki! Dial 911! Hurry!"

They ran as fast as they could, and soon enough, the police came and so did an ambulance with an emergency medical technician. They questioned me for about twenty minutes, and then let me go back to my house.

I strode back to my house and tiptoed inside to my room. I grabbed a paper towel and wiped all of the grass clippings from my feet. I wondered who those two girls were. To take my mind off it, I wrote some music. Writing music always made me feel better.

"Tighten" by Camber Yppah

I'm going to pull on your heartstrings
I know it's going to sting
Heart as cold as ice
And you know I will always be like a vice
Tighten, tighten
Tighten, tighten
Strange noises in the night
And you know we'll always be in a fight
Tighten, tighten
Tighten, tighten
We'll always have that day in the rain
But of course, we only gave each other pain
Tighten, tighten
Tighten, tighten

Chorus:
Every once in a while, I loosen up
Take a Coke and fill up a cup
I take a look back
At our old knickknacks
I then decide for myself that
I'm always going to be like a vice
Tighten, tighten
Tighten, tighten

You were always the main attraction
And I was always the big distraction
Tighten, tighten
Tighten, tighten
We used to be ordinary Joes
But now we are international foes
Tighten, tighten
Tighten, tighten
I talk more trash than a radio
And you kept trying to turn my volume down low
Tighten, tighten
Tighten, tighten
(chorus again while music fades out)

41

"Manners" by Camber Yppah

Before you did that crime to me
I didn't know our relationship would be history
Pardon me
Let me be
I use my manners to charm
And you use your manners to harm
Pardon me
Let me be
Your manners were like poison to me
Not to care but to please
Pardon me
Let me be
When you hug me, it's like paying a fee
So costly
Pardon me
Let me be
Suddenly, you broke up with me
Stole my house key
Pardon me
Let me be
Nine months later you called me
With a plea
Pardon me
Let me be
You tried to say sorry
But then you played me
Pardon me
Let me be
Kelly is her name
And she's buying your little game
Pardon me
Let me be
Our time is up for manners
And my love is better than hers
Let me be, and please pardon me!

"Take Her Home" by Camber Yppah

Can we dress up?
Sip from teacups?
She's been asking
We've been basking

42

In our own childhood regret
How come you don't even fret?
She's ready for a date night
To see with her own sight
It seemed like she was just four years old
But she grew older and even more bold

Chorus:
She broke my comb
Take her home
Take her home
You can't leave her alone anymore
Take her home
Take her home
Now she's not easy to adore
Take her home
Take her home

Now your sister has a mister
That kissed her, ooh
She was a plain Jane
Just trying to find out the rules of this game
We call it life
(chorus again until fade)

"They Say They Love Me" by Camber Yppah

They say they love me
Flowers and kisses
Can't make up for the wishes
That were lost
When they tossed me out
Like a runt, short and stout
They say they love me, but I have my doubts
I don't scream, I don't pout
I just shout, my heart out

Chorus:
Rain, I hear you drizzling
Is there something that I'm missing
Maybe the sun will clear the darkness away
Let it delay

43

Maybe I was born
To mourn
They say they love me
Could it be true
Is it a clue
They say they love me
I say they don't
(chorus again to fade)

That's just a few of them. I love writing, but even writing cannot help me unsee what I witnessed tonight. Those two girls could have lived fulfilling, happy lives, and now they were gone. I grabbed my phone off my nightstand and played serene sounds so I could calm down and fall asleep. There's a concert I have been saving money for, and I was planning to ask my mom if I was allowed to go when I woke up in the morning. *Good night.*

When I woke up in the morning, my hair was in frizzy curls and my clothes clung to my sweaty body. Emersyn, Aloki, and I promised each other we wouldn't tell Mom and Dad about last night.

I waltzed into the kitchen, and my mom chirped, "Morning, sweetcakes."

Emersyn and Aloki were at the table, munching on overly-burnt and thickly-buttered toast. Mom took a big gulp of pulp-filled orange juice (I know, gross), and I tried to work up the confidence to ask her about the concert. I finally cleared my throat and said, "Mom, I am sixteen now, and I am very mature for my age. I've been saving money the last couple of months to go to this concert in town tonight. I would be going with Dyanne, Adi, and Gabi. You know they are trustworthy."

My mom bit her lower lip and answered, "I'm sorry but you can't go to the concert. There isn't going to be anyone to supervise you. I do not want you or your friends to end up dead in a ditch somewhere."

I got furious and retorted, "Well, their mom has enough money to go, but I know you hate her for some reason, which I will never understand. Even if you had the money to come, you would probably find an excuse not to come. You're a nasty witch."

Mom looked appalled but said nonchalantly, "Now because of your mouthiness, you earned yourself a grounding of three days."

"But Mom!"

"That's final!"

"Ugh!"

I trudged back to my room without a word and dialed Dyanne, Adi, and Gabi. Adi answered. "Hello?"

I replied, "It's Camber. Just calling to let you know I asked my mom about the concert. She said since there is no parental supervision, I can't go."

Adi said, "I have an idea. You have that huge window by your bed. Dyanne, Gabi, and I will come by that side of the house to help you sneak out. Be at the window, ready to go around six thirty. Gabi will be driving, so we'll see how that goes. Bye!"

I hung up and felt a bit mischievous. To pass the time, I decided to write some more songs.

"Midday Sun" by Camber Yppah

You caress my lips when I smile
I always feel the urge to dial
Your number
But sometimes, you hurt me
Bruises and cries
I am surprised I have not died
From you

Chorus:
Aromatic smells and grass stains propel
All over me
You stare at me in the daylight
You try to lift me up to the sky just like a kite
But let's run in the midday sun
While we are still young, let's try to have some fun
My friends tell me not to trust you
But sometimes I don't want to do
But let's run in the midday sun
While we are still young, let's try to have fun
I'll forget all the bad things you've done
(chorus again until fade)

"Don't Say That I'm Free" by Camber Yppah

Don't do that to me
Don't say that I'm free
I'm chained by your locks of hair
And entrancing stare
Why do you do that to me

Chorus:
Don't do it
Don't don't do it
Don't don't say it anymore
When you know my freedom is poor
You know that I'm right
So don't make it a fight
Don't say that I'm free
When you call me baby cakes
It's like getting bit by multiple snakes
Don't say that I'm free

I must make that decree
(chorus until fade)

I looked at the clock, and it was two in the afternoon. Holy shit, I spent two hours writing. I decided that I should start getting ready early. I looked through my closet and found a floral dress that matched my white heels. I brushed my hair until all the knots were gone, and then I recruited Emersyn to French braid my hair in fear that the knots would soon return. Emersyn asked, "So, where are you going all dolled up?"

I lied. "I am just going to be staying in my room tonight."

Emersyn accepted my answer, tied my hair, and left the room. I started browsing through my makeup, trying to find a cute look for tonight. I applied some mascara, a tan lipstick, and some light eye shadow.

I listened to music, cleaned, and did other chores in my room to pass the time. I looked at the clock, and it said it was 6:38 p.m. I snatched my crossbody purse with my concert money off my bed. I opened my window, and I spotted Dyanne, Adi, and Gabi. Dyanne saw me and yelled, "Camber! Jump and I will catch you."

I thought she was crazy, but then I remembered that she was a powerlifter. She'll be able to hold me, but it's my job to jump toward her. I flung myself out the window as gracefully as I could, and with a scream, I fell into Dyanne's arms.

She let me down, and Gabi urged us to hurry. "C'mon, I'm driving, and I do not want to be late."

We all piled into the car, and it smelled like dog biscuits. Dyanne, Adi, and Gabi are sisters, and they have five dogs: Emelea, Olisa, Sheyanne, Shiane, and Sheyannin. When we were about twenty minutes away from my house, I saw a deep ditch and thought I saw something move in it. At first I thought it was an animal, so I asked Dyanne to stop the car in case it needed help. Gabi brought the car to a halt, and I got out. I came closer to the ditch and saw that it was not an animal. It was a girl about my age.

The girl looked like she was covering herself with the mud from the ditch. I tried not to get dirty because I had some decent clothes on for once. The girl didn't notice me at first; she seemed like she was off in her own little world. I introduced myself. "My name Is Camber. What's your name?"

The girl answered in a rusty voice. "My name is Arden-Syden Biana, but most people call me Arden. Thank god you stopped!"

I asked, "Why are you in the ditch? What is going on?"

She explained, "My parents have been torturing me since I was little. I am suffering mentally and physically. I finally escaped the hellhole that they call a home, and I came here so that I would be disguised in the mud. I do not have any more energy to run. I'm in real danger. If they find me, I am dead."

I felt nauseous thinking about everything Arden had to go through. I thought for a moment. What if Arden came with Dyanne, Adi, Gabi, and me? While we went to the concert, she could stay in the car with locked doors and air-conditioning. But what do we do with her after that? Before I could respond to Arden, I saw a man and woman sauntering slowly toward us.

Arden screamed, "That's my parents, Camber! You have to protect me! Please don't let them hurt me!"

I didn't care about getting muddy anymore. I dragged Arden out of the ditch and put her in Gabi's car. I instructed Gabi to lock the doors, and I would explain everything later.

I gulped, wondering if there would be a later. I didn't want Arden's parents to hurt anyone ever again. I approached Arden's parents. The woman said, "My name is Gwynne, and this is my husband, Onyx. We want Arden, and then you can go about your business."

I replied, "I am not handing her over. She told me the abuse she had to go through. You two are sick individuals. I will not let you hurt her."

Onyx lunged at me and covered my mouth and nose. I clawed at his arms, fighting for breath. I started to fade away, and I could see the light as bright as ever.

CHAPTER 6

LAIKYNN FINNICUM

I was watching my favorite reality television series when a news alert popped up at the bottom of the screen. Local girls, Dyanne, Adi, Gabi, and Camber went to go to a concert when Camber spotted a girl in distress at the side of the road. The girl was another local, named Arden-Syden Biana. Arden-Syden was discovered to be suffering from years of abuse and neglect from her parents. Soon after Camber found Arden-Syden, her parents showed up and smothered Camber to death because she helped Arden-Syden get away. The parents were found to be Gwynne and Onyx Biana who are both going to trial soon.

I shuddered at all the crimes that have been happening lately. I turned the television off with one click of the remote, and I dawdled into the kitchen. My sisters, Haylen and Ainsley, were finishing up their dinner at the kitchen table. My mom, Vimala, was slowly mixing up her coffee with a stirrer, and my dad, Weston, was skimming through the sports page of the newspaper.

My mom sighed and pulled me into the hallway closet. She said, "I have something important to say to you, and I couldn't risk Haylen or Ainsley hearing. I already told your father. Okay, so you know how your Auntie Bilwa and cousins Pankhi, Mabel-Lyn, and Kathei are tight with money? Well, they robbed a bank. The police have not found them yet, and I am worried that they are going to set us up. Your Auntie Bilwa knows that you, me, Haylen, and Ainsley look like carbon copies of them. What if the police convict us? I don't know what to do, Laikynn."

I tried to take in everything that my mom had just said. I replied, "Mom, everything will be just fine. They know better than to resort to larceny. If the universe is holding off on them going to jail, maybe it is for the best. Everything happens for a reason. Karma will be back to bite them eventually. Now, come on, Haylen and Ainsley wanted to have a movie night with you."

My mom smiled and came to the kitchen with me. Ainsley exclaimed, "I wanna watch *Bambi, Annie, Pinnochio,* and *Beauty and the Beast.*"

Mom responded to Ainsley, "Sure, I guess that's why I stocked up on so much bagged popcorn. Haylen, are you ready to get your movie on?"

Haylen nodded, and I asked, "Mom, since Haylen and Ainsley are going to stay up late, can I stay up too?" Mom nodded her head, making her brown curls bounce.

I went upstairs with a skip in my step, and reached my bedazzled bedroom door. "Achoo!" I sneezed and a glob of snot sprayed all over my door. I grabbed a disinfectant wipe and started scrubbing my door until it was clean. I opened my door and right away caught a whiff of something rancid. The smell seemed to be coming from the bottom of my bed, so I shimmied under there and found a moldy piece of cake. I had never seen that before in my life, so don't ask me how that got under there. I shut my door and pulled my sparkly, gray socks off my feet. I flung them over by the laundry basket and missed. Oh well, I'll get them later.

I plopped in my comfy swivel chair and stared at my metal desk that was in front of me. I grabbed a pink gel pen and started chewing on it. I got out some paper from the desk drawer and stacked it neatly. I had asked to stay up late so that I could plan my future. I love doing stuff like that, so I decided I would do that tonight. I took the pen out of my mouth and started to write.

Who will I marry?

Yasiel Puig, of course! He is quite an amazing baseball player, and he could teach me how to pitch a baseball! We will adopt twelve kids, and there will be six boys and six girls.

What should I name the kids in this little fantasy?

Girls:
Carmela-Garden-Whipple-Poseyanne Rwoedda Puig
She will be enrolled in lyrical dance classes
PaysleeSou-Chorina-Melores-Pyper-Jae Brijitte Puig
She will do cross country
Cyrkle-Lyrik-Jemima-Jil-Luelle Maricarla Puig
She will do acrobatics
Tigi-Leire-Thomasin-Tigar-Dawnie Peyge Puig
She will play softball
Cidney-Kennocha-Mattliyn-Mattison Rihliee Puig
She will play clarinet
Mily-Ta'tyana-Trysta-Trinity-Pacience Blissala Puig
She will play soccer

Boys:
Beatrix-Guardian-Peter-Maisyn Stu Puig
He will play basketball
Porter-Lester-Elmore Toraki Puig
He will play football
Oakley-Ralph-Terelle-Jaysin Lou Puig
He will play the piccolo
Khole-Bryin-Rittevin Arlee Puig
He will play baseball
Waine-Lyle-Hector Minho Puig
He will play the oboe

LIST OF PETS WE SHOULD OWN:

- (2) DOGS – CHAMPION AND SNOWBALL
- (1) cat – Princess

- (1) *guinea pig* – Enoch
- (1) *hermit crab* – Pinchers
- (1) *bunny* – Tawnya

All of the animals would be in my room at night so that the children would not fight over which animals sleep in whose room.

I gave my hand a break because it was cramping up. I got up and washed my hands because my hands get very sweaty when I write. I headed to the kitchen to get an ice-cold glass of Sprite for refreshment, and I passed Haylen, Aisnley, and Mom snuggled on the couch. Popcorn was surrounding the couch, and the movie was as loud as it could go just like how every Finnicum likes it. They each had their own separate bowl. Haylen was shoveling popcorn in her mouth, watching the movie so intently, you would think that she would never be able to take her eyes off it. Mom was drifting in and out of sleep every now and then, fighting to stay awake. Ainsley was in a deep sleep with her head in her popcorn bowl. I felt bad because it had been her idea to have the movie night in the first place.

I grabbed a tall glass and the tray of ice cubes that we had in the freezer. I poured my soda into the glass and gave myself four ice cubes. I put the tray away, and when I went to pick up my glass from the kitchen countertop, I saw that I had made a *culaccino* mark from the condensation. I saw that there was a note on the refrigerator from dad. It said that he had to make an emergency trip for one of his clients, and he would not be back for a couple of days.

I turned around and saw Haylen with an empty bowl. It startled me that she was able to be so quiet. Haylen had her hair in a top knot by the crown of her head and confessed, "Laikynn, I didn't want to say anything, but I heard what mom told you earlier. I told Dad that I had to use the bathroom, but instead, I followed you and mom. I'm scared."

I said in a calming voice, "Hay bales (her favorite nickname), it will all be okay. Don't worry yourself over that. Please, we have this under control."

I heard a loud bang on the door. Then another, and another. The banging sounded angry, and I was too frightened to answer the door. I stood in front of Haylen and slowly inched toward the door. I yelled, "Door's open!"

I had hoped that it was just a neighbor. I came around the bend to see who was at the door, and it was a police officer. Oh my lord. The police officer smelled like cheap cologne and fast-food grease. He said in a macho-manly voice, "I'm looking for Bilwa, Pankhi, Mabel-Lyn, and Kathei Hazeldine. I have reason to believe they live here. In fact, you are a perfect match for the description of Kathei Hazeldine."

I shook my head and said, "Sir, I am not she. My name is Laikynn, I am innocent." My stomach went sour with the nervousness I had welling up inside of me.

The police officer replied, "I don't believe you." The officer had a booming voice, and it probably woke up Ainsley and Mom because they came traipsing to the kitchen.

"Ah," the officer started, "I have the whole crew now. All the Hazeldines. C'mon, you are all going away for a long time."

Ainsley, Haylen, and Mom looked terrified, and I was so frozen in fear. I panicked. Dad was away for his emergency client, and when he gets back, we will all be gone. The officer handcuffed mom first, and I watched in horror as he handcuffed Ainsley and Haylen. They winced with pain at how tight the officer fastened the cuffs. Soon enough it was my turn. The officer instructed, "Follow me. If you run, you can answer to my taser."

Ainsley started crying and went out the door with mom, each of them tightly hugging the other. Before going out the door, Haylen said to me abruptly, "You are a liar. You said everything was going to be okay."

She went out the door with tears dampening her whole face. I didn't know what to say to her. I also didn't know what was going to happen tonight. Why do we have to look like carbon copies of our cousins? I dawdled out the door, not wanting to leave. I shimmied into the back of the police car, and the officer shut the door. I thought about my dearest friends.

Illiana and Aubrianna are twin sisters with a lovable fashion sense and amazing personalities. Marieta is a dancing fool who acts like such a ditz sometimes. February was as cold as her name, passing secrets from person to person but seemed to be the friend in the group that was always there for us. Last but not least, Sawyer is quirky and always carried her flute with her. She liked the idea that people thought of her as spontaneous. Sometimes, I wonder why they are my friends. I have always felt like the friend in the group who was a bother, and even if I went to jail, I don't know if they would be worried or not.

I am afraid of our family hearing about this and getting upset. Mom, Dad, Haylen, and I are the only people who know the truth besides Auntie Bilwa and her daughters. We'll have to tell Ainsley soon enough. When we arrived at the jail, the officer locked all of us into one cell, and I went to the one corner by myself. How could he do that? Lock us in this cell without proof? We were not even dressed in jail uniforms yet, and I wasn't sure what was happening. The cell was dank, grimy, and the toilet smelled to the high heavens. There was one long, sleek bench with vandalism where my mom and Ainsley sat. Ainsley was sobbing with her head cradled in mom's lap, murmuring something about being afraid.

Haylen walked over to me, and I was sure that she would pick a fight. I didn't mean to lie to her, truly. She said to me in a mature tone, "I hate liars. You understand that more than anyone, Laikynn. But I know you didn't know that the officer was coming. I have been such a drama queen about this. I don't hate you. I am just so stressed out and horrified. I am sorry that I projected my feelings on you."

I responded, "I forgive you, and I understand. I love you. I should have told Mom to include us all in the conversation. I just didn't want you and Ainsley worrying. I had no idea that we would end up here, and we still have to tell Ainsley what's going on. I want to escape this place."

It looked like a lightbulb turned on in Haylen's head. "That is a great idea actually. I'm sure Mom has caught Ainsley up on everything. I have a plan. Ainsley, you, and I can escape through the air duct up there." Haylen pointed one of her scrawny fingers up toward the ceiling. "We'll climb through it, and it should lead to the roof. We'll safely climb down the jail and make a run for it. Then—"

I cut her off with a shriek that made my voice crack. "What about Mom? We can't leave her here!"

Haylen explained, "Mom would never go along with this. We cannot involve her in this escape. We can go home and get a hold of Dad. We'll explain the situation and see what he can do to help."

I nodded my head in agreement. I studied my nails and saw that my orange nail polish was chipping off. I thought for a second, and before Haylen scurried away, I opined, "Mom is asleep. I believe we should do this escape now or we might not have this kind of opportunity again."

Haylen looked over where Mom and Ainsley were sitting. Mom was over there, snoring away. Ainsley was awake, so Haylen dragged her over to me, and we filled her in on the plan.

Ainsley said, "I will only do this if Mommy can come with us."

I assured her. "Ains, we will get her out of here, I promise. We need to get out so that we can help Mom out later." Ainsley accepted my answer, and I bent down to hug her.

I explained, "To get into the air duct, we will need to climb. Haylen will get on my shoulders and get up into the duct. Then, I will have Ainsley on my shoulders, and Haylen, you'll have to pull her up. Then you will pull me up, all right?"

Haylen bobbed her head. She was not heavy at all on my shoulders. She got up in the duct, and then it was Ainsley's turn. She was lighter, so it was easier getting her up there. I was just worried that Haylen would not be strong enough to get me up there. Haylen grabbed my hands and pulled me halfway into the duct. I told her to let go, and I pushed myself up the rest of the way. The duct smelled of freshly-sharpened pencils and old, dusty books. The duct was clean and speckless, which struck me as odd.

It was as if they cared more about the cleanliness of the duct rather than the cleanliness of the jail cells. Ainsley and I shimmied behind Haylen until we saw an opening. It led to the roof, so Haylen's plan would work after all. We happily got on the roof, but we didn't realize how high it would be, nor how hard it was to see. We held hands and stuck together, but Ainsley made a fatal misstep, and we fell together. It was a long and scary fall until we hit the cement. I saw the light as bright as ever.

CHAPTER 7

◢ ◣

AVONLEA PIRCY

I wake up in the morning with a cold sweat and shivers, the effect of a terrifying dream. Fire rose up with screams, and burning flesh was everywhere. I was in a strange place, nothing like I had ever seen before. I was in a house, and the room I was in was not burning. I wondered what it all meant. I dangled my feet above the off-white polyester carpet. My fake nails made clicking noises as I rapidly texted my friends. One of my friends, Ophelia, was complaining about how her mom didn't understand her, which is such a cliche teenager thing to say. I peregrinate over to my walk-in closet and pick out a sassy, strapless, cherry-red crop top with black leggings. I sauntered over to my bathroom.

My bathroom was the worst part of the house. The Formica was peeling, and the enamel in the sink was starting to chip away. There was a leak underneath the sink, and black mold was growing behind the toilet. My parents had promised to hire someone to repair everything, but they have been too busy to actually go through with their promise. I slipped off my comfy, baggy pajamas that had polar bears on them and slid on my day clothes. I ran my hands through my hair, emulating a comb, and I tied it up into a messy bun. I doused myself in strawberry-scented perfume and applied some deodorant.

I sat on my bed, brushing my toes against the soft floor. I heard a knock on my door. "Come in," I said.

It was my mom, Athulya, and dad, Attila. My parents sat on my bed with me, and my mom told me, "Your dad and I heard something really depressing on the news, and I thought of you and your sisters. Three girls escaped from a jail . . . I mean they tried to. They went on the roof and slipped. They all passed away. I just thought that I should tell you and acknowledge how much we love you. We do not want anything like that to happen to you, Hananiah, or Brynlee. Even though we don't know all the details of the story, I am sure they had a loving family that is devastated right now. We love you, Avonlea." My mom and dad were in tears, and I started crying too. We were bear-hugging for about ten minutes, and then they left my room.

I took a tissue and dabbed away all my tears. I checked my phone and saw that Ophelia had texted me in a group chat with my other friend, Aymeline.

Ophelia: Do you girls feel like misbehaving tonight?

Aymeline: Sure, why not? We are always getting perfect grades, and everybody thinks we are these poster children for responsibility. Why can't we have fun for once?

Ophelia: Avonlea, what do you think?

I thought for a second before answering. I had no idea what she was proposing.

Me: What exactly would we be doing?

Ophelia: Let's get drunk.

Me: Drunk? Are you crazy?

Ophelia: No, but you sure seem to be a little chicken.

Aymeline: Aw, poor baby.

Me: I guess I'm in. So, where and when is this happening?

Ophelia: Let's say, 7:30 p.m. at my house. My parents have some fancy overnight yoga retreat with their yuppie friends.

Me: What about your sisters?

Ophelia: My sisters? Puh-lease. They are two and four, Avonlea. They'll be out like a light, and we can drink in the garage.

Me: Okay, bye. See you then.

Aymeline: Bye, losers.

Ophelia: Hasta luego.

I cannot believe what I just agreed to doing. I cannot let anybody find out. For an hour I paced around my room, trying to figure out what my story would be, what I should tell my parents when I ask to go to Ophelia's house. I decided the easiest thing to do was to tell them it was a simple sleepover, that the night would consist of watching movies and eating snacks. I looked at the clock, and it told me that it was three thirty. I had four hours until I went to Ophelia's house. I decided that I would write a letter to my cousins because I haven't seen them in a couple of years. All our schedules are pretty busy, but I figured that since I had time, I better do something meaningful.

Dear Loralee, Bryan, Julianna, Patrick, and Alayna,

I haven't seen you guys in forever, and it is driving me crazy! How is Uncle Kip and Auntie Meritt? How are all of you?

Loralee ~ How is your friend Anneliese? Are you two still playing pranks on Alayna and Bryan?

Bryan ~ Are you still playing the cornet?

Julianna ~ How's your cat, Avery? Still a snuggler?

Patrick ~ Are you still with Makaela?

Alayna ~ Hey, girlie! Do you still remember our old handshake?

Sincerely,
Avonlea Miyah Pircy

I folded up the sheet of paper and tucked it into an envelope. I taped it shut with Scotch tape and wrote the address in flowery letters. I face-palmed. What I wrote was so vague and impersonal. Of course, they are not going to be the same. I'm sending it anyway. I just hope to God it doesn't offend them. Maybe they would appreciate that I was trying to reach out.

It was four o'clock. I put a stamp on my letter and sashayed down to the kitchen to get something to eat. I always ate like a bird, picking at the crumbs and nibbling at the edges. I took a cake out of our fridge. It was an undersea-themed cake with teal fondant. My dad bakes in his free time, and he is very good at what he does. Cake was my guilty pleasure, so I took a hefty slice.

I took a fork and shoveled the cake into my mouth. My taste buds were roaring for more. Soon, I finished my piece of cake and tossed my plate in the trash and my fork into the sink. I started washing my hands and daydreaming about a life in which I didn't have friends who pressured me to drink. I dried my hands off with a dish towel and realized that it was twenty till five. I went into my living room and my sisters, Hananiah and Brynlee, were in there. The television was off, and Hananiah was reading a thick, multichapter book. Mom and Dad were nowhere in sight, and Brynlee was playing tea party with her dolls.

I took the remote and turned the television on with the purple power button. I started flipping through channels until I found an old, classic Disney movie. Brynlee didn't mind, but Hananiah grunted and left the room. I should've known not to turn on the television while she was reading. I watched the full movie, and after it was over, the clock said that it was a quarter till seven. I was getting extremely antsy. My nails were bitten down to the quick. I started biting at their frayed remains. Brynlee looked up at me with her sweet little eyes. She stared at me a little longer before asking, "Is everything okay, Avonlea? You only bite your nails when you're anxious, and I know for a fact that Hannie didn't make you anxious."

I thought for a moment about telling her the truth, but even though she is one of the most trustworthy people I know, I couldn't risk my secret getting out. I decided to lie. "I was biting them because I was too lazy to clip them."

Brynlee looked at me quizzically, but then she just went back to playing with her dolls. I sat there until the analog clock declared that it was seven o'clock. My mom came in the room with various snacks: carrots and French onion dip, celery and peanut butter, and strawberries.

"Avonlea, have you been eating? You look like a toothpick. Please eat up," my mom stated.

I responded, "I ate today, but thank you. I was wondering if you could take me over to Ophelia's house. Her parents are out of town, and she needed some company other than her sisters. Can I go?"

My mom answered enthusiastically, "Well, of course! C'mon, let's get in the car!"

I thanked my mom, and before leaving, I gave Brynlee a big hug. I saw Hananiah sitting in the kitchen, and although we may not always get along, I gave her a hug and told her that I loved her. Mom and I hopped in the car, and within twenty minutes we arrived at Ophelia's. I got out of the car and waved goodbye to my mom as she backed down the driveway. I walked up to the garage door nervously with my legs trembling. I opened the door, and Ophelia and Aymeline were sitting in green, fold-out chairs waiting for me. I saw endless cases of vodka, beer, wine, and so many other alcoholic beverages. I sat down in a rocking chair beside them and asked, "Oph, where did you get all of this alcohol?"

She replied, "My dad has a whole cellar of alcohol, and he has no idea that I know about it."

Aymeline grabbed a beer from one of the cases, and I gulped as she handed it to me. It tasted foul in my mouth, and I felt like I was going to get sick. I finished it and smashed the can under my right foot. There was something about deviation that made me want to drink more and more. I drank so many different beverages I lost count after a while. Ophelia kept partying along with me, but eventually Aymeline grew very worried about us. I drifted off to sleep, and I saw the light as bright as ever.

CHAPTER 8

ALL TOGETHER NOW

- Mehreen Kenna
- Rhyann Kenna
- Seraphina Kenna
- Kiely Cosmosis
- Mckai Cosmosis
- Annyn Cosmosis
- Chesney Oasischei
- Preity Oasischei
- Larken Oasischei
- Aunt Katrielle
- Aunt Mila
- Ksenia Blackwell
- Hannalyn Blackwell
- Camber Yppah
- Laikynn Finnicum
- Haylen Finnicum
- Ainsley Finnicum
- Avonlea Pircy

My name is Cezyn. All of these women and girls died tragically. I wasn't part of a chapter, you didn't skim past me. I am the gatekeeper of a different place. One that you have never heard of, and might never have the pleasure or misfortune of knowing. As you can clearly see, one decision, whether it be big or small, can cause a chain effect. So, I urge you, especially with all that is going on in this world right now, be kind. In everything you do, be the best you can be. The human spirit wins, as soon as we band together and decide to help each other.

Printed in the United States
By Bookmasters